# Atlantic Hotel

Other titles by João Gilberto Noll available
from Two Lines Press:

*Quiet Creature on the Corner*

# Atlantic Hotel

*João Gilberto Noll*
*Translated by Adam Morris*

TWO LINES
PRESS

*Hotel Atlântico*
© 1989 by João Gilberto Noll
Translation © 2016 by Adam Morris

Two Lines Press
582 Market Street, Suite 700, San Francisco, CA 94104
www.twolinespress.com

ISBN 978-1-931883-60-3

Library of Congress Control Number: 2016955682

Cover design by Gabriele Wilson
Cover photo by Cardinal/Getty Images
Typeset by Sloane | Samuel

Printed in the United States of America

1 3 5 7 9 10 8 6 4 2

This book was published with the support of the Brazilian Ministry of Culture / National Library Foundation (obra publicada com o apoio do Ministério da Cultura do Brasil / Fundação Biblioteca Nacional) and by an award from the National Endowment for the Arts.

 MINISTÉRIO DA CULTURA
Fundação BIBLIOTECA NACIONAL

**ART WORKS.**
arts.gov

I went up the front steps of a small hotel on Nossa Senhora de Copacabana, almost on the corner of Miguel Lemos. As I ascended I heard nervous voices, somebody crying.

Suddenly, a bunch of people appeared at the top of the stairs, mostly men who looked like cops, perhaps some military police. And they started coming down with a gurney.

On it was a body covered by a patterned sheet.

I halted on a single stair, glued to the wall. A woman with a bleach-blonde dye job was coming down the stairs, crying. She had that tic—jerking her mouth in the direction of her right eye.

I regretted having walked into that hotel. But as I stood there, retreat only seemed another cowardly act I'd have to shoulder on my journey. So I pressed ahead.

When I found myself standing in front of a girl behind a counter, who was attending to guests, I couldn't contain a sudden burst of laughter. I hadn't guffawed like that since I was a kid. The girl surely must've thought I was some kind of relative or friend of the corpse, laughing from shock, and with a look of dismay she waited for me to finish cackling.

Someday I'll end up in a coffin, too—so I took the girl's hand as soon as I stopped laughing and kissed it. With her hand still between mine, she slackened her face, as if a gesture like a kiss on the hand were completely commonplace and even natural at a hotel reception desk. Her long expression opened into a faint smile: "Would you like to speak with a guest, sir, or would you like a room?"

"A room with a bathroom, double bed, TV, and a desk where I can lean on my elbows and think."

"I have just the thing," she said, her gaze already completely intoxicated.

"It wouldn't be the room where the crime…" I ventured.

"I wouldn't do that to you, sir…" She looked at my hands and asked, "Your bags?"

"I stored them at the airport." It was the first thing that came to me.

"Oh, well, for guests without bags we ask for a three-day deposit," she explained, with courtesy that tingled the back of my neck.

I filled out the registration card, lying that I was married—I pictured a woman waiting for me someplace in Brazil, and ventured that having her waiting would awaken the receptionist's curiosity about me.

The girl at the reception desk had black hair, thick bangs; her hair came down past her ears. She looked like a flapper. And black eyes, big.

She pressed a bell and a boy appeared. The boy was dressed in a gray uniform with gold buttons. She asked him to take me to room 123.

Then she gave me one last disarming look. That was when I really started to get interested.

The boy guided me through a long, poorly lit hallway, stopped in front of number 123, opened the door with a certain gravity. I commented on the murder. He barely let out a *humph*. Asked if I had any baggage. I repeated that my bags were stored at the airport.

The boy closed the door. When I sat on the bed, I heard a hoarse moan, as deep as an animal's.

Then came another moan, so I took a pillow and smashed it against my ears. I thought maybe I was just jumpy, full of palpitations. Then I tossed the pillow away and shook my head violently.

The moaning kept on. It was masculine and coming rhythmically. I touched myself—a little bit excited. I picked up the phone and waited for reception to answer. The flapper picked up.

"I'm the guy that just checked in, and I'd like a whiskey neat—but I'd like you to bring it yourself."

She told me she'd be at my room in two minutes.

When she came into the room with the bottle of whiskey and a glass, I said I'd fallen for her in a matter of seconds. She said she didn't believe me. I asked her to touch me and see for herself. She took hold and told me it had been a long time since she'd met somebody so ready to go. I was already unbuttoning her blouse.

As soon as I had her undressed, she got down on all fours atop the filthy green carpet immediately. I kneeled behind her. My mission: to mount from outside her field of vision. No touching above the waist, just anonymous haunches seeking each other out pathetically.

Late that night I went out to find someplace to eat. I raised the collar of my blazer and went whistling a made-up song. The month of June was ending and an incredibly cold wind blew through Copacabana.

On the corner of Barata Ribeiro, a newsstand displayed the paper with a headline about the extraordinary cold in Rio that year. As soon as I read the headline, I realized I'd lost my appetite and that a sort of nausea had installed itself inside me.

I went up the hotel stairway feeling an immense fatigue. Now the person at reception was a boy, who was listening to a battery-powered radio. I remembered to ask if they figured out who the killer had been in the murder at the hotel. He told me they'd given a suspect on the radio, a Uruguayan doctor.

Upon entering my room I noticed a nearly invisible bloodstain on the carpet. I crossed over it and threw myself on the bed with all my clothes still on. I didn't even take off my shoes.

I was exhausted but couldn't sleep. I tossed and turned; I stared at the light already peeking through a slit in the curtains. I thought about my departure, about how long I would last.

I got up and opened the curtain. What I saw wasn't dawn, but fully ripened daylight. I hoisted the sash. The window looked out on the backs of various buildings. In one of the windows a woman was filing her nails. The smell of coffee in the air. Leaning on a sill, a boy watched a pigeon's short flight. The pigeon landed in a gap in the wall meant for an air conditioner. I noticed there was a nest there, with a little baby pigeon inside. The pigeon that just landed, which must have been the mother, pecked her baby with her beak.

I drew the curtain. A countdown was in progress: I needed to get going.

But I decided to go back to bed. I kicked off my shoes. I felt that I was repressing a sense of hopelessness inside myself, because I had to get going soon—so I pretended to be calm, very calm.

If I feigned madness, or maybe numbed amnesia, the world would rush to commit me.

And isn't that the same thing as going away? But with the advantage of not having to expend any effort, such as coming and going from dumps like this one. If I went crazy, they'd have me doped all day and night, asleep as soon as my head dropped in a haze.

I leaned over the edge of the bed. The almost invisible bloodstain was still there. A gunshot... why not?

Yes, I would kill too, and earn a cell and free board from the state. Maybe resume drawing, which I gave up in adolescence. Draw all day long if the other prisoners let me. At night I'd fall asleep so that the next morning I could awaken and continue the interrupted line from the day before.

Maybe that way I'd get back to finding joy in just killing time. Eva, a blonde I'd been mixed up with for the last few months, was always telling me, "What you need is a normal occupation."

When alone with myself, in front of the mirror, I'd started saying, "Unoccupied, that's what they call you."

"Unoccupied!" I shouted inadvertently.

And my heart beat faster, fearing the whole hotel had heard and would come knocking on my door with that human curiosity I usually did whatever I could to avoid.

A few minutes passed and nobody knocked. I picked up the phone. The woman at reception had already arrived. With a languid tone, suggesting complicity, she asked what I wanted. I said I wanted her; I was dying of stress.

"I beg you to come to my room this instant."

"Sure, I'll come take a look to see what's going on, sir…and what should I call you, sir?" she asked.

"Love. Call me Love, the Word Incarnate," I replied.

It wasn't long before she was there, unbuttoning her blouse, offering me her plump breasts, which I began to gobble, bite, taste. I said that this time I wanted to fuck her face-to-face and, lying on top of her, suck those magnificent tits.

"This time I'll get you pregnant, and as soon as you give birth I'll come get the kid and take him with me," I said breathlessly.

By the time I finished speaking she was sitting on the edge of the bed; I was standing. As she brought me closer to her mouth, with ravenous flair she said, "No, no, our son is this right here."

"All right, go ahead, be good to him," I said, dripping from every pore.

When the receptionist left the room, I sat down on the bed. I felt as if she'd taken something from me. I felt flatter, half-scared, one small noise was enough to send me to the bathroom to see if there was somebody hiding there. On my way into the bathroom I saw how panicked I would look to any intruder.

I left the bathroom slowly, trying to normalize my breathing. I opened the curtains, looked up, and saw a bit of the sky of that blue day. I took off my blazer.

I turned to face the room. Once again I noticed the bloodstain on the carpet. I switched on the radio. A friend from adolescence, one I hadn't seen in more than twenty years, a singer, was talking about his passion for Schubert. Then he sang one

of Schubert's Lieder. When it was over, the inter-
viewer tried to ask something but the singer said
no, he had nothing else to say, only that he owed his
decision to become a singer to Schubert. I sat back
down on the bed.

I glanced at the time: eight thirty. It took some
effort to get up; my legs hurt. I slipped my blazer
on and went to the bathroom, steadying myself on
things, feeling a sort of disability—the image of a
convalescent getting ready to leave the hospital
came to mind.

In the mirror I saw deep circles under my eyes,
skin all scaly, parched lips. I slid my tongue along an
inflamed cavity in one of my teeth, figuring it wasn't
doing me any good to stay here enumerating the
signs of my body's deterioration. The time to leave
had come.

I turned on the faucet, splashed water on my
face, hair, neck. An alarm clock rang in the distance.
Right after that, a school bell rang. The nervous
horn of a car. And in the background, the muffled
rumble of Copacabana.

When I appeared before the woman at reception, I noticed that something intrigued her. She squinted and asked why I'd suddenly taken on this aged look.

"Well, in fact," I replied, "I can't hide that a few minutes ago something happened that left me this way."

"What was it?" she asked, startled.

"Look, my angel, I think I'm about to go find out," I replied, trying to recompose the swaggering air I usually maintain around women I've taken for a roll in the hay.

She gave me back the money corresponding to the two days I'd advanced for arriving without bags. I said goodbye, and told her we'd see each other again one day, feeling completely ridiculous.

I went down the hotel steps half stooped, my legs and back were killing me. When I got to the door I put one of my hands against the wall to hold myself up, and with the other I pressed against the pain in my lower back. Maybe I should go back to my room? I wondered. Maybe I should stay, give up? Maybe I should marry the flapper from reception? Maybe I'll be content with the company of a woman?

I'm old, I thought. Old at barely forty. Traipsing around would be madness. Legs, weak. Irregular heartbeat, I know. And my rheumatoid posture…

There, stopped in the hotel doorway, I felt vertigo. Foggy vision, out of breath…

But I needed to get going. I stepped down from the stoop and leaned against the wall of the building. Lots of people were passing along Nossa Senhora de Copacabana, just like every morning, some brushed against me, touched me inadvertently, coughed.

I felt on the verge of fainting but avoided the idea of asking for help. Resorting to another person's assistance would be the same as staying, and I needed to go.

Then I thought about getting a taxi. So I went looking for one. I walked by moving one leg at a time, steadying myself on other people like a drunk. Until my feet stepped into the dark puddle in the gutter. I hailed a cab and it stopped.

I told the cabbie I was going to the bus station. I got in the back, curled up, lying down on the seat. The driver asked if I was sick. With what remained of my voice I said I was only tired. Bus station, I repeated. The cabbie kept talking, but I couldn't follow.

At one point I understood he was talking about the cold. I said: Oh, the cold, as cold as the Russian steppes. He told me: The Russian steppes are cold as death. This I heard quite clearly.

I returned to my senses. The traffic. The cabbie commenting on the smog in the Rebouças tunnel. I leveraged my hands against the seat back and managed to bring myself upright. The car was emerging from the tunnel.

I was almost better, just a tremble in my hands.

"How come you're so tired?" the cabbie asked.

"I was partying all night," I replied.

He laughed. I showed him my hand and said, "Look how I'm trembling, it's alcohol tremors."

"You're an alcoholic?" he asked.

"Yeah, but I'm going to a treatment center in Minas," I replied.

He shook his head, gave a little snort of assent, and said, "I have a brother-in-law who drinks. He was in rehab three times."

Suddenly, the cabbie said we'd arrived at the bus station.

"You all right?" he asked.

"Great," I replied, almost startled.

I watched the commotion at the bus station and saw the hour of my departure had arrived, the way someone going under for surgery witnesses the anesthesiologist's first procedure.

I took a wad of money from my pocket, opened my hand, and gave it to the cabbie. He asked if

I wanted change. I inquired if he knew where to find the ticket counters for the buses to Minas. He smiled, gave me a look, and said he had no idea.

"I'm sorry." I said it full of a sudden shame.

"Sorry for what, man?" he asked.

"Sorry for being who I am," I replied, closing the car door softly.

I got on the escalator going up. The one coming down was jammed with people. Between the up and down escalators there was a long concrete staircase. People in a hurry were going up and down, skipping steps.

On the escalators everyone seemed totally immersed in what they were doing. Noticing this relaxed me. I too would manage: travel, take the bus, arrive somewhere else.

There were long lines at the ticket windows. A lot of people were milling around. Many others sat on benches. A man and a woman kissed shamelessly at a lunch counter. A man left the pharmacy looking at his watch.

I sat on a bench, way at the end. The rest of the bench was full. I stretched out one of my legs a bit, without letting my heel come off the floor. My leg looked a bit pitiful. Maybe it was the crumpled up unwashed sock, the fleck of mud on my shoe. A pitiful state I'd done everything I could to disguise. I brought the leg back over beside the other.

Now I was looking at nothing except the dirty floor on the upper deck of the bus station. Gazing at that dirty floor, I had nothing else to think about. Maybe a vague yearning for a child's intimacy with the floor.

It struck me that my journey might bring me back to that intimacy. A voice inside me said, between excitement and apprehension, *Who knows, maybe I'll end up sleeping on the ground.*

I took out the ball cap I always carried in the pocket of my blazer. I put it on my head in the position I liked, a little to the right side. I no longer needed a mirror to be sure the cap was placed in exactly that position.

The cap obeyed, loyal. My hands had memorized the way to execute their task. As always, when the task was completed, I gave a little tap on the cap's brim to see if it was really on right.

I ran my hands down my body as though searching for something and felt a bulk in the blazer's other pocket. It was a thick piece of paper folded several times—a map of Brazil I'd bought two days earlier.

I looked around, making sure there was room to open the map all the way. I put my legs over the armrest of the bench. Now, with nobody on either side, I could extend my arms.

As I opened the map I remembered what I'd said to the cabbie. That I'd be going to alcohol rehab in the Minas countryside.

On the map, the Minas countryside looked like a swarm of little towns. My gaze descended a little, crossing into São Paulo State and stopping on Paraná.

I was thirsty. I thought about getting a mineral water. I folded the map, discreetly tucked it under my butt. Then I got up and walked away.

I didn't even make it five steps. A woman seated on the bench facing mine called out, "Hey, sir, sir, I think you forgot something there."

I looked back, toward the spot where I'd been

sitting, saw the paper folded on the bench seat, turned to the woman, and shook my head, saying, "It's not mine."

I decided to buy a ticket to Florianópolis after I saw the name of the city on a ticker above one of the counters. Why not try out an island? It was a situation that interested me. And besides, I'd never been there before. I lifted the collar of my blazer, which had slipped back to its normal position. I touched my cap. I needed to consider how cold it would be down south.

When I found myself with a ticket in my hand I felt like I'd just purchased my own freedom. But a feeling of too much liberty invaded. Like I wouldn't be able to make it on my own. The bus wasn't leaving for two hours, so I sat down to kick around a few ideas.

"Calm down, kid," I murmured.

I noticed a little boy was looking at me very close by, smiling. The little boy came even closer and asked, almost laughing, "You talk to yourself?"

Then somebody's hand appeared and starting

pulling the child away. The little boy kept staring at me, laughing. I lowered my eyes.

I got on the bus and saw that my seat was at the end of the aisle, next to a very pretty blonde. Typical blonde girl's freckles under her eyes. She was wearing a black sweater and blue velvet pants. Her seat was next to the window.

I said excuse me and sat down. She said sure, and I noticed a foreign accent. After the bus got moving I pretended to look out the window, but was really staring at my beautiful foreign neighbor. The question of what country she was from remained.

I turned my head to face forward, commenting with a distracted air that it had been abnormally cold in Rio. She said she never expected temperatures below twenty degrees in Rio de Janeiro. And the wind, she added. I said yes, the wind—and looked at her looking at me. Now that I was certain of her accent, I asked, "You're American?"

"I am," she said.

"Where from?"

"Boston."

"And this elegant Portuguese?"

"I've been to Brazil several times already. This time I came back with better Portuguese. I'm an archaeologist. I came to coordinate some excavations."

"Excavations?"

"Yes, excavations to search for the possible existence of a pre-Colombian civilization that's still practically unknown."

"Any good leads?"

"We've every reason to think so."

Her name was Susan Flemming. She had big green eyes. She told me she was traveling by land so she could get to know the interior of Brazil.

We went hours without talking. When a beautiful sunset began to take shape, something came to my lips—I don't even know what. I did make out her response: she didn't think so.

We remained silent for another half hour. Suddenly, she said it was getting dark. Then, running a hand through her hair, she said this time of day always devastated her. A knot in her throat that formed only as night fell.

She asked me to excuse her for confessing such

personal things to a stranger. I said I was an actor, a man accustomed to the intimacies of others.

I glanced at her profile. She was now just a shadow against the moonlit night.

She picked up the blanket that was folded in the seatback in front of her. It was getting colder. I also took the blanket out from in front of me. I told her I had very little with me for warmth, just my blazer. As soon as I got to Florianópolis I was going to buy a good wool shirt. She remarked that Canada had beautiful wool shirts.

"I lost my daughter in Canada," she said just like that—abruptly.

And she stopped, as if she'd gone too far.

"You lost your daughter in Canada?" I asked.

"She died in Canada when she was seven years old," she replied.

Susan then paused briefly before adding, "Another reason for this trip, to forget."

I told her I didn't have any children. That, although I'd toyed with the idea of wanting them, the thought of having to feed and clothe someone for such a long time suffocated me. Feeding and clothing myself was enough of a problem, one I no longer expected to solve.

She laughed. I said I liked her laugh.

Then I took her hand. And we fell asleep.

We awoke to the voice of the driver telling us we had forty-five minutes to eat dinner. The bus glass glared. I crossed my arms as a sign of the cold, mentioning once again that I didn't have much to cover up with except my blazer. Susan bent down and opened a bag she had under the seat. She took out a wool coat with a hood.

"Here, put this on, it's what's left of my ex-husband since we separated," she said, chuckling.

I sat there awkwardly; said something that didn't rise above a mumble.

"He never wore it, but I like to wrap up in it to read. Take it, I have other things to put on," she said.

We got off the bus. The night frozen. It must have been southern São Paulo, northern Paraná.

In the restaurant bathroom I saw myself in the coat. It was red with a yellow fringe on the hood.

We sat in the back of the restaurant, which was

empty. We ordered steak and fries, a bottle of wine. I said the coat actually looked good on me, kept me nice and warm. She said Peter and I had more or less the same body type.

We were both slightly embarrassed by this comment. I imagined an American a little taller than me wearing the coat. He was blond, wrapping Susan in a long embrace.

We returned to the bus. A child was sniveling. We decided that from then on, if we wanted to talk, it would have to be in whispers so we wouldn't keep anybody from sleeping.

"Talking in whispers, like in a convent," I observed, whispering.

"There's a legend that tells of ancient people here in South America," she said, also whispering.

"What does the legend say?" I asked.

"It says that speech was eliminated from their religious rites. They didn't pray from their mouths like we do. For them the gods only appeared through the absolute surrender of the spoken word."

"We've come a long way," I said.

And we both laughed, covering our mouths with the blanket to muffle the sound.

Then we hugged. A prolonged embrace.

"Oh, this embrace," I murmured.

"Are you a poet?" Susan inquired.

"Just an unemployed actor, at the moment living off the sale of my car," I replied.

And we laughed some more, covering our mouths with the blanket again.

When her laughter tapered off, Susan proposed that we try to sleep. It wasn't long before I heard her deep breaths. I couldn't say why, but I suspected she was pretending to sleep. Would we stay together in Florianópolis? I wondered. And I fell asleep.

When I awoke, the bus was parked in front of a restaurant by the side of the highway. Susan had gotten off. It was hard to see exactly what was outside—there was a strong snowstorm.

When I got off, I felt what seemed to be frost on my skin. As I made my way to the bathroom I saw Susan leaving the restaurant by a side door.

There was a detail to her exit from the restaurant

that I couldn't understand: she was wearing dark glasses. In the middle of a snowstorm in the dead of night, here was this American woman in dark glasses.

I kept moving and went in to take a piss. But I couldn't get it out of my head. I left the bathroom, paid for a mineral water at the register, and went to the counter to wait for the water. Throughout this trajectory I felt watched. Difficult to explain: a sudden chill on the nape of my neck. I looked behind me. Two men and a woman drinking coffee. Further on, an old man walking with difficulty. The girl at the cash register giving a boy some change.

I drank the mineral water. I sighed, and thought that this would pass when I got to Florianópolis. I figured the long bus ride was leaving me exhausted, seeing things.

I left the restaurant making calculations about where we must be. "This is the border between Paraná and Santa Catarina," I heard one girl tell another. They were coming into the restaurant, giddy from the road. Laughing and horsing around.

There were three, four buses stopped. Some passengers were sleeping inside them. A little before getting back on the bus I distractedly stumbled over a stone painted white. I stopped, wiggled my foot to see if it was hurt. No, my foot was fine.

Susan was already in her seat. Still in dark glasses. When I sat down, I could tell she was sleeping. Rather deeply, it seemed. She had a strange snore. I thought nobody else on the bus would be able to sleep with her snoring like that. It was too intense, too pathetic for anyone nearby to shut an eye.

Susan's head fell forward. I straightened it against the headrest. I wondered again if we'd stay together in Florianópolis. Then I thought I'd relax, maybe even have a little nap.

To my surprise, I not only had a nice snooze, but also a beautiful dream. The best part: I woke up with the dream still clear in my mind. I was a woman sitting atop some dunes. A breeze was blowing, such that I could feel the heat of the shimmering sand. I was a woman from the twenties.

But unlike the films of that era, nothing was in black and white. Almost everything was a shade of gold, but with pink splotches.

I was wearing a metallic bracelet. Every time I

looked at the bracelet I saw it give off flashes from the sun.

I was very hot. My dress had a plunging neckline. I slipped a hand down and touched my breast.

In the distance, low on the horizon, leagues away, a man in a white suit was approaching, perhaps in a light-colored hat too, his body fluttering as he came—an effect of grains of sand moved by the wind before his image.

When I opened my eyes the first thing I thought was to tell Susan about my dream. So I turned to the side, and saw that she had some kind of viscous substance dried into the corner of her mouth, on her chin, staining her black sweater. A dark yellow that her system had expelled overnight. It didn't really look like vomit, but a more serious secretion.

Her mouth was open, tongue hanging out. I removed her dark glasses. Her eyes were wide, pure panic. I replaced her glasses immediately. I took Susan's wrist, released it, had no idea what to do.

Discreetly, I covered her face. I needed to think. I looked out the window and saw a blue morning, hills full of dense vegetation. A child's voice said we must be getting close to Florianópolis.

I leaned back in my seat. I noticed a black bag had fallen to Susan's feet. I picked up the open bag and inside saw several packages of barbiturates, antidepressants, antipsychotics: every sort of remedy to halt the perturbed mind. The boxes were all open and empty. Some torn from top to bottom in desperation.

Susan must have taken these pills back in the restaurant where I found it strange to see her in her dark glasses, I figured, rattled at the thought of it. She hadn't wanted anyone to notice the first transformations of her eyes, hence the dark glasses. I continued to reason as though I had a moral obligation to understand her plan all the way through its outcome.

Later, when I had returned to the bus, she had already been deep into that terrible snore and was certain never to reawaken—I concluded hurriedly, so that the nightmare would soon be over.

The bus was crossing the bridge to Florianópolis.

In moments we'd pull into the station.

I waited until there weren't any other passengers nearby before I checked on Susan's body one last time. I pulled off the blanket and her glasses; her face remained the same: the mouth and eyes agape. I felt for her pulse, then covered up the body once again.

No doubt about it: Susan was dead. I realized that this was the second cadaver I'd encountered in fewer than forty-eight hours. The other was the one from the hotel in Copacabana.

The bus was empty. I wondered if they were already getting suspicious about how long it was taking us to get off.

It agonized me that I might be suspected of something. But it was already too late to undo my mistake. I'd spend years being dragged through the courts, facing down the sordid affairs of the justice system, too drained to believe my own innocence.

I got up. I went slowly down the aisle, thinking about how to make myself invisible as I got off the bus. I didn't want anybody to notice me.

I walked around the bus station for a while, not knowing what to do. It occurred to me suddenly to look for a window that was selling tickets to Porto

Alegre. The next bus was leaving at midnight. It was a long time until then.

I continued wandering around the station, hoping to hit upon an idea.

I went to the bathroom. That was when, in front of the mirror, I realized I'd gotten off the bus with Susan's ex-husband's coat.

"With Peter's coat," I recalled, realizing only after I'd said it that I'd spoken aloud to the mirror.

A mustachioed man washing his hands next to me said, "What's that?"

I told him I'd just said that it was the first time I'd been to Florianópolis.

He said he was born and raised in Florianópolis, but lived in Curitiba now. When I sensed he was going to ask where I was born and where I lived, I said I was a salesman. That I got to travel the whole country in my line of work.

"So there are salesmen who cover the whole Brazilian market?" asked the mustachioed man.

I told him I didn't know of any others.

We left the bathroom together, the mustachioed man and I. He asked, "And Acre, for instance, have you been there?"

I assented, said goodbye, told him my bus was about to leave. I picked up my pace, leaving the mustachioed man behind.

Suddenly I stopped. I was at the front of the station bookstore. They sold a nice variety of magazines and newspapers as well. I was just going in to leaf through some things when I noticed a man in a gabardine coat behind one of the spinning postcard racks. What caught my attention were the dark glasses he was wearing, the same as Susan's.

The man was turning the rack. I'd stopped, perturbed by his glasses.

To calm myself down I picked up a book: a best seller set during World War II. I read the first page, then looked around. The man in the dark glasses had already left the bookstore. I returned to the book, relieved.

The hero's tale went like this: the story begins when he, a British spy, Catholic, enters a church in Paris, and in the church he thanks God for the grace of living in a time when it's clear whom one ought to fight: the enemy.

In the next scene he's with a lover in a hotel in Nice, raising a glass of champagne as he says, "Long live the enemy!"

I shut the book. Leaving the bookstore I saw that people in the station were avidly discussing something. Then I saw what it was all about: from the doorway of the bookstore I could see the bus I'd gotten off a half hour before. A big crowd was gathered around. Suddenly everyone turned to a tall, bald man who'd just arrived. A newspaper reporter took a photo of the bald man, who seemed to be asking to get through the crowd.

I thought I'd better get out of there. There must be at least one reporter who'd be interested in the person who'd sat beside Susan during the journey. I walked along the station's storefronts until I found an exit.

A very cold wind was blowing. I pulled up my hood. It was a magnificent day, with that deep blue of a winter sky.

I walked into the wind, freezing my nose. I found what must have been the old city market. To protect myself from the wind I wandered for a while through the market.

I stopped from time to time at a stall, asking the price of something just to hear the sound of my voice, killing time until lunch.

I thought I'd look for a bar where I could sit and have a cognac without so much commotion. I left the market, confronting the wind once more. I turned down a narrow street, then a narrower one. On this street was a little bar, with four, five tables. I sat down and ordered a cognac.

The guy at the bar was very blond and seemed

like he was from the interior—German territory. I showed him my empty glass, and within seconds he had poured me another shot of cognac. That was when I asked if he knew of anyone driving in from the coast, to western Santa Catarina, someone who might want to split the cost of gas.

It just slipped out: it could have been any destination. What mattered was that I needed new bearings on my journey.

The guy said no, not to western Santa Catarina. But he had a brother who was driving to Rio Grande do Sul the next day, somewhere in the north or northeastern part of the state—he wasn't sure. The brother was getting married to a southern girl. They were driving in the brother-in-law's car—the brother of the bride.

"When's the wedding?" I asked.

"Two weeks," the guy replied.

He told me his brother was going early because he was moving down there. He was going to work for his future father-in-law.

"But yeah, I don't know of anybody who's going to western Santa Catarina…" he concluded suddenly.

I ate lunch in a restaurant located on a wide beach. I heard the waiter massacring English as he tried to talk to a pair of German tourists. He was telling them that the church on the edge of the plaza was the city cathedral.

I ate fish and drank white wine. Between bites, I admired the German couple or confirmed once again that the cathedral indeed had an immense staircase. When I turned back to my plate and my chalice of wine, I felt I was experiencing the rudimentary parts of a delusion.

In the afternoon I meandered around downtown. I bought a postcard of the Florianópolis bridge. I had a habit of collecting postcards as souvenirs. At the time I already had a couple in the back pocket of my pants, all crumpled up. One of them showed Copacabana beach at night. On the other was the ferry to Niterói. Now the postcard of the Florianópolis bridge, spanning a scandalously artificial blue sea, would keep the others company.

Toward late afternoon, I thought I'd better find a hotel. I went two blocks down toward the sea, and on a corner I found a hotel in an old but well-preserved house, painted dark green.

I asked for a room with air conditioning. I closed the door to the room, but then remembered I'd never operated an air conditioner before. I pulled a chair in front of the unit. I started to fuss with the buttons, to see if I could overcome my chronic ineptness with machines. I had to mess with it for more than five minutes, but I was successful.

Then I lay down on the bed, just enjoying the temperature. I switched on the radio, and was surprised to hear Francisco Alves singing. Then the announcer came on, saying it was a whole show dedicated to Francisco Alves.

I took off my clothes while still lying down, thinking about taking a bath. Even naked I wasn't cold.

I sat up on the bed and faced my white body in the mirror. I stood up, went into the bathroom, and turned on the shower. I began lathering up, thinking I'd go to the movies that evening.

Wrapped in a towel, I opened the minibar and took out a can of beer. I remembered my dream on the bus, in which I was the woman observing a man who had just appeared on the horizon. I let out a small burp, and a little bit of sour beer came back up into my throat. I took another slug of beer. I realized that this had not been the first and would not be the last dream in which I was a woman.

Francisco Alves was singing a sad waltz. The lyrics were a lament that his beloved was in love with another.

I lay down again. I recalled the flapper from the hotel in Copacabana. Unwrapping myself from the towel, I closed my eyes and opened my arms as if to make of myself an offering.

I stayed like that for a few minutes.

But a sudden rebellion came over me. I bit my hand, my arm, and started to moan and roll across the bed until I landed on the shaggy carpet.

"I'm dead, bury me!" I exclaimed.

I looked myself over in the mirror hanging in the small hotel's foyer. I was wearing my ball cap, but since the doorman told me the temperature would fall sharply that night—the wind would begin to send things flying—I pulled the hood of the coat up over the cap.

In the mirror I looked like I was from a foreign land: a person who was obliged to confront the worst possible weather every day. I felt the lack of something I'd never need to tolerate. I lowered my eyes.

Out on the street a frozen wind did indeed begin to gust against me. I stopped a few times, steadying myself on posts, and considered returning to the hotel.

Suddenly I saw the movie theater and decided to go in. They were showing a stupid American comedy titled *Conquests of a Single Man*. The actor was pretty; I'd never seen him before. The actresses were all likewise unknown to me. There were several, all of them having affairs with this guy at the same time.

The end of the movie showed the guy crossing the Golden Gate Bridge in a red convertible with the only ugly woman in the entire film. The theater reeked of piss. I got up. The lobby seemed welcoming as I crossed it. There were some people sitting around, waiting for the ten o'clock show. I made my way to an empty spot on the corner of a sofa. I sat down and rubbed my hands to prepare for the cold outside. There was violin music playing in the theater.

When the people from the eight o'clock show had all left, the people in the lobby started getting up and filing calmly into the theater.

The usher closed a red curtain across the theater's doorway. Then he looked at me and said they were starting the last showing. At that moment, various lights in the lobby went out. A shadow fell on the room. The woman who had been selling tickets came out of her little booth and put on a headscarf, tying it under her chin.

I thought of saying something to the usher, maybe telling him I'd already seen the previous showing, and I was just killing time before meeting a friend at ten thirty. But when I fixed my gaze on the place from where he'd been speaking to me, he was no longer there.

So I got up. And went out into the fierce night wind.

As I left the theater a can was being dragged along by the wind. My breath grew labored again, and I could only think about finding the fastest way back to the hotel. But as I came to a corner, bent into the wind, I looked to the right and saw the bar where I'd had a cognac that morning.

I went in. The same blond guy was there. He saw me, pointed to an empty table, and said, "So, sir, you remember how my brother and his brother-in-law were going to Rio Grande do Sul tomorrow?"

"Yes, what happened to them?" I asked, taking a seat.

"Oh, nothing… That's them over there. The guy that's blond like me is my brother, and the darker one is his brother-in-law," said the bartender, pointing to a table with two young men.

"So that's them?" I said.

Then I asked for a cognac, and imagined, if the wind let up, I'd try to find a woman.

The wind was blowing hard outside. The bar gave off a cozy feel that only enveloping atmospheres within a cold night are capable of transmitting. People were sitting around, looking at each

other with the air of ones who have the simple priv-
ilege of not being exposed to the elements.

Out of the corner of my eye I noticed that the
two guys who were going to Rio Grande do Sul the
next day were staring at me, the darker one definitely talking about me like I was somebody to be
excited about for some reason.

I turned back to my cognac. I thought each of
the two brothers, who looked like they were from
the German territory, had the miens of complete
innocents, totally opposite from the black-haired
guy, who was perhaps a bit older—he, even from
afar, came off much more sly.

The black-haired guy got up. He came over to
me and asked, "You wouldn't be the actor from that
film *The Man Who Wanted to Be God?*"

"That's me," I said.

"Well, I saw it, but I didn't really think it was
any good," he said, striking a cavalier air.

"No kidding," I said.

He asked, "You ever work on a soap opera?"

"On three, but never in a lead role," I replied.

"Oh yeah…?" he blurted.

"I've done some films and quite a bit of theater," I added.

"But not anymore?" he asked.

"Not exactly," I told him, "Nowadays I'm on the hunt for treasure, or something like that."

"Ah, you're a man of mystery, like me," he said, showing some camaraderie for the first time.

But then he did something I didn't like at all: he sat down at my table without asking.

"So yeah," he said, moving in close like he was about to tell me a secret.

"So, yeah," he repeated, and then went on, "My buddy that works here tells me you're interested in going to western Santa Catarina."

"That's right," I replied.

"So yeah, I have a car and tomorrow I'm going with my brother-in-law over there, the brother of my buddy here at the bar. We're heading to a little town in Rio Grande do Sul, not too far, where he's going to marry my sister."

"So then…" I said.

"So then come with us. I'll drop off my brother-in-law in the little town and we'll keep going to western Santa Catarina if you want. We'll make a deal on the price of my time—I could use a little extra dough."

I didn't know what to say and kept tracing the rim of my cognac glass with my finger.

Just like that, the guy was offering me a complete itinerary, something I wasn't used to contemplating. But then there was the way his attitude made me suspicious—he seemed at least as cunning as everybody else in the bar put together. But, on the other hand, what was I sticking around for? *Somebody is offering to be my oarsman across this river,* I thought with relief.

"So?"

"Why not?" I replied.

The car was a yellow Gol, not very new. We left Florianópolis in the afternoon. The brother-in-law of the groom was driving, I was in the passenger's seat, and the groom was in back. The brother-in-law was named Nélson. The groom, Léo. I found it strange that neither of them had asked about my bags.

Nélson flipped on the radio. We were leaving the

city. Léo talked about how he'd been in Florianópolis for a year and a half, he'd come from western Santa Catarina, a village called Belo Si. In two weeks he'd get married and start working with his father-in-law in a little town called Pomar, where the wedding would be, and which he was about to see for the first time.

I asked Nélson if he'd been born in Pomar. He said no, he was adopted by the family of the girl who was going to marry Léo. He was from a town near Pomar called Luzes. The family in Pomar adopted him when he was two years old.

A little after nightfall, Nélson stopped the car. The highway was dark and deserted.

Dogs barked nearby. Nélson leaned back in his seat and said, "I thought it was right about here... Oh, there it is, that's the entrance."

"Entrance to what?" I asked.

Nélson burst out laughing, started howling, cruising down a narrow paved path bordered by eucalyptus trees.

In front of us I could see a two-story mansion, long and wide, painted white, it seemed, in the moonlight. As he parked the car, Nélson stopped howling, looked at me, said, "Well, tonight's the night, my actor friend, tonight we get to have our night of glory. The most fantastic women in Santa Catarina are all here. Tonight's gonna be very special for my new little brother-in-law, Léo. I promised to bring him here before the wedding. So tonight's all his; I reserved the best women, all on my tab. One last bachelor fuckfest.

After delivering those seemingly memorized lines, Nélson gave Léo a rather firm jab to the chin and started howling again.

As we walked from the parking lot to the mansion we passed alongside a grated metal fence with huge guard dogs behind it, crazed by our presence. They were so furiously worked up that they barely failed to clear the metal fence as they leaped at us. Word had it, Nélson told us, that one night one of the dogs got out by accident and ripped a client to shreds.

"They say the whole thing ended there, because to this day nobody's ever breathed a word about the guy's disappearance. They say he was a loner. I heard the girls buried the body nearby."

The mansion was in the middle of a patch of woods, which in that darkness appeared to be quite dense. A beautiful woman opened the door and exclaimed, "Is this him?"

"That's right, the most eligible bachelor around!" Nélson bellowed.

We went in, passing through a spacious foyer with a curved staircase that most certainly led up to the bedrooms. We went into a large parlor full of tables. They were all empty.

A woman with Asian features sat in a corner, up against the bar. Behind the bar, a bartender in black tie stared vacantly into the empty room. When he saw us he smiled, and started convulsing a tapered shaker.

The woman escorting us, in jeans and a yellow sweater, said things were falling off day by day.

"With the exception of one or two travelers passing through, we have practically no work during the day. Lately things are only picking up around eight in the evening."

"Then it's a good thing the house has the side businesses, the lumber and that lumpy cemetery...

Instead of gravestones, it's just all grass and discreet little crosses stuck here and there," Nélson explained, his eyes popping.

Then the woman escorting us said she'd go call her colleagues, and went through a door beside the bar.

I looked at Nélson and said that a night in this place must cost a pretty penny. He said he was the boss of the place. All the women here owed him big time.

"It took my blood and sweat to get this business going back in the day. At seventeen, eighteen years old I ran away from home and came here to do dirty work for the girls."

Nélson spoke in enigmas. But all the words he was saying, the house, it all seemed to me like something out of an old film.

Léo was drinking cognac, sitting on a chair marooned in the middle of the dance floor. He seemed nervous, chewing a straw.

I told Nélson I was going to get a room and try to sleep a bit. That I was tired, needed some rest, just recently over a wicked flu.

"No, don't be like that, my actor friend," he replied.

"I've got to, Nélson, I'm twice your age, if I don't take care of myself I'll fall apart," I said, looking him straight in the eye.

The woman who'd received us reappeared with two very young girls.

"I brought these two for you," she said to Léo.

And the two girls sat in Léo's lap, one on each leg. Léo blushed. *An old film*, I murmured.

The Japanese girl remained seated at the bar.

I closed the door to the room they gave me and turned on the light. A double bed was pushed up against one of the walls. A TV. A white curtain, lacy. The door to the bathroom was half open, an armchair near the window.

It was rather cold—there wasn't a heater. I turned out the overhead light, felt my way over to the lamp beside the bed, and turned it on. I sat on the bed, took off my shoes. Then I lifted the thick comforter and got underneath without taking off my clothes, not even my cap. I thought that nothing about this room made it seem like a brothel.

I lay on my side, turned to the wall, just like

they say Indians do when they sense they're about to die.

I noticed a newspaper near my feet, bunched up against the wall. I squirmed down to reach it. It was a local paper. That day's date. On the first page there was a notice about an American's suicide on the bus from Rio to Florianópolis.

The newspaper said Susan had lived for some time in a depressive state, caused by the drowning death of her seven-year-old daughter.

Next to the article was a photo of Susan—her passport photo by the looks of it—faded.

The article explained that the information regarding Susan Flemming the paper received was relayed from an employee of the U.S. embassy in Brasília.

They made no mention of Susan's profession. Didn't cite any relation to an archaeological dig in Brazil.

I tossed the newspaper. I grabbed one of the pillows and hugged it.

I fell asleep.

I awoke to someone knocking on the door. It took me a while to recognize my surroundings. They knocked again. I said they could come in and rolled over to face the door.

It was the girl with Asian features I'd seen sitting by herself at the bar. She opened the door and said, haltingly, "Nélson sent me here. He said you'd be needing some company."

She stayed where she was, with the doorknob still in her hand, almost smiling.

I told her Nélson was mistaken, that I was dead tired.

"Later, maybe," I said, signaling for her to close the door.

"Let me sleep," I demanded, my voice hoarse. But she didn't obey me. She closed the door and came over to the head of the bed, asked if maybe I was sick, if I was sure I didn't need her.

Then she sat on the bed at the level of my knees, touched my feet, and said I should take off my clothes, put on fresh pajamas—nice-smelling, she'd get me some.

"You wear pajamas?" I asked, underlining my

voice with an angry tone.

"They're not mine," she responded, "they're my father's. They're what I took from him when I left home three years ago."

"Let's see these pajamas." As though giving the order in my sleep.

In seconds she came back with the folded pajamas, and they actually did smell rather nice. You could smell them an arm's length away. She waved them lightly under my nose and asked me if they weren't just what I needed. I told her she was completely right and curled up, feeling blanched.

Then she pulled off the covers and started to undress me, piece by piece. She had a way of doing it that got me to help. The last thing she took off were my socks. Then she started to dress me in the pajamas.

With the pajamas on I turned back to the wall, the same position I'd been in when she arrived. She sat down beside my feet.

"If you want you can keep the pajamas," she said.

"I'm not bringing anything with me," I said.

"That's what I'm going to start doing," she said.

"What?" I asked.

"I'm not going to keep anything with me any-more," she replied.

Then she remained silent for a while. I almost didn't move. I was staring at the wall like an Indian who senses he's about to die.

Suddenly, I broke the silence myself, just to see if she was still there.

"Is your family Japanese?"

"My parents both have Japanese parents, they live in Londrina, in Paraná. That's where I ran away from three years ago. I hitchhiked all the way down Santa Catarina, sometimes doing whole stretches on foot, until I ended up here. I'll stick around an-other six months.

"And then where will you go?" I asked.

"I'm trying to save up some cash, I'll meet a friend of mine in Miami, she's doing really well there. I'm going to try, too."

I asked her to turn out the light.

When I awoke the next morning I was still turned to the wall. It was a white wall, but darkened by dampness in a few places, turning gray if not black.

I heard Nélson's voice. He had to be nearby, and was practically shouting as usual. One bit of what he yelled came through completely clear: he would no longer associate with weaklings. That, once he left for Australia, he didn't want a single idiot in his field of vision. He would build an empire with two or three people as decisive as himself.

"Think of Onassis, a guy who washed up in Argentina when he was still a kid living hand-to-mouth. Well, he ended up marrying America's widow!" He was saying this as though speaking to a crowd.

At this point, Nélson began to make burlesque shouting noises, sometimes howls like the ones I'd heard in the car as we arrived at the brothel. I let out a sigh that did me well to hear aloud. I concentrated on letting out another, but it didn't work, it wasn't reproducible.

So then I got up, opened the lacy curtain, and saw the day. Out in front there rose some craggy-looking hills. To the left, if I looked out the corner of the window, low, dense plants stretched into the distance.

There were no clouds. I opened the window, letting the sharp sun in. The weather promised to be warmer. Wind was blowing again, creating some movement on the surface of the trees' leaves. I didn't shut the window.

My clothes had been placed tidily on the armchair. I went into the bathroom, shut the door.

On the back of the door I saw an old calendar, 1986, from something called Fichter Transport. On the top part of the calendar was an image of Christ. Christ stripped of his robes, just a cloth around his thighs. Standing, his hands tied together with rope, his crown of thorns, drops of blood on his forehead. His pupils gazing on High.

Someone was coughing up a lung on the other side of the wall. Suddenly, they hawked loudly and flushed the toilet. I took a piss and then a bath. This brothel even left a toothbrush wrapped in sealed plastic. The soap, shampoo, all serviceable.

I came out of the bathroom wrapped in a towel. Nélson was lying on my bed—shoes on. One of his legs was bent, the sole of the shoe right on the mattress.

"So how's it going," he asked, "Isn't that Japanese girl great?"

"She has a great mane," I replied, not sure what I meant by it.

"A great mane," Nélson repeated, and stuffed his hand down his pants.

"Get yourself ready to go, we'll be in Pomar before lunch," he said, getting up.

And he left the room with his hand down his pants.

I got dressed. One of my socks had a hole in it, exposing my big toe. I hastily yanked on the part with the hole to cover my big toenail, which needed trimming.

On this leg of our journey Nélson was flooring it. I was sitting in the back now. There wasn't much other traffic on the highway; only rarely did Nélson have to pass a truck.

Léo didn't say much. Nélson told me his mother died in childbirth.

"I was the child, the only one she had. I heard she died because of the doctor's carelessness. If that doctor's alive, I'll kill him, just a matter of figuring out who it was. I still haven't found the right guy."

"And your father?" I asked.

"They say my father was the son of Arabs—Lebanese, something like that—I guess he sold carpets. He knocked up my mom and then took off."

After that Nélson got quiet. And then after going around a curve he came to a stop in front of a gate. On the gate was written: OASIS FARMS.

Léo got out of the car and opened the gate. The car passed through, stopped. Léo closed the gate, got in the car. The car started down a dirt path.

Many wild horses roamed an expanse. They were playing, running, lying down flicking themselves with their tails on a light slope in the field. We'd already been going for about five minutes along the dirt road. I was just looking, silent.

Then I saw a huge structure made of dark wood ahead. It looked like a barn. The car parked in front.

Nélson put the car keys on the dash. He said they were going in to take care of a quick piece of business with a friend, and if I wanted I could go down that path over there to the left, there was a pretty river down there. We'd meet up on the shore of the river in five, ten minutes max.

Three police dogs chained to an iron stake at the entrance to the wood structure were barking like crazy.

"Rambo, shut your mouth," Nélson yelled.

The biggest dog shut up. The other two quieted down little by little.

"Rambo's the boss, he commands the other two," Nélson explained, turning to face me.

Nélson and Léo went into the wooden structure. I decided to go down the path to the river.

The path was wet, full of stones and exposed roots. On certain stretches I needed to steady myself on tree trunks so I wouldn't slip.

The river at the bottom of the path was actually worth the trouble. It was clear, just a few strokes to the other side. I leaned down, dipped my hand in the water—the river was so clear that I could see the blue of the sky reflected in the water. A school of little fish passed by so quickly I barely had a chance to look at them.

I started to walk along the shore. The sand was

thick and rocky. I stopped a few times to throw a stone in the river and felt myself sweating under my clothes. It was getting hot.

I hadn't walked ten minutes when I saw blood on the sand. I stopped. I saw that the blood continued to the right, leaving a trail into a thicket.

I followed the blood for a while. On the far side of the thicket I stopped. I heard voices.

I bent down and impulsively grabbed a weighty stone. I stood there waiting to use it. It was heavy, but an instinct I didn't fully comprehend at the time told me to keep holding the stone in my hands for a while.

Suddenly, as if to prepare myself, I heaved my arms up, but got impatient waiting for I didn't know what, so in a fit of hysteria I threw the stone onto the trail of blood.

The voices, which had silenced, returned. This time closer. It didn't take me long to discern they were the voices of Nélson and Léo. Nélson was speaking softly now, but was clearly arguing with Léo.

I'd started to walk back the way I'd come, darting my eyes all around with each step, when I saw the two of them on the other side of a boulder, which reached almost to the water on a particularly muddy stretch of shore.

I ducked back and hid behind the rock. Through a fissure in the rock I could see what was happening.

Nélson put the barrel of a revolver against Léo's forehead. Léo was shirtless, on his knees in the mud.

Léo was crying. Nélson was sputtering, "If you don't kill him right now I'll finish you! The guy's a soap opera actor; if he wanted to, he could rat on us to the police just to get famous again! How was I supposed to know this would happen? And he saw, there's no doubt about it, he saw!"

I saw what? I thought. Was it the blood I saw? Was that what Nélson wanted to hide by killing me?

How to escape?

The veins in Nélson's neck were popping out more than usual due to the effort he was making to keep his voice down.

"The guy's wandering around here somewhere, go find him and kill him, go on—if you don't, I'll kill you and then tell all of Palomar it was me who popped your girlfriend's cherry, you little bitch! My dear little sister, yes her, I was the first guy to fuck her when she was twelve years old!"

Nélson pulled Léo's head by the hair, and forced him to kiss his crotch, "Kiss it, kiss the guy who paved the way for you, little bitch, kiss it!"

I started to creep away from behind the rock, back up the riverbank. When I got to the top I'd run as fast as possible, since the dogs would definitely bark like mad. I'd have to be as fast as possible because the barking would put me in the sights of Nélson's gun within seconds. As fast as possible I'd run and get the key from where I was certain Nélson had left it on the dashboard—I'd make a getaway in the car. I'd escape.

I dragged myself up the riverbank, taking hold of exposed roots to hoist myself up. The ground had the wetness of dense overgrowth that never sees any sunlight, leaves sticking to my clothes as I climbed, everything muddy, moving carefully so I wouldn't make any noise—when I got to the top of the bank there'd be no other cover, I'd have to run for it, make noise, get quickly to the car, which was close to the guard dogs who would bark as though possessed, pulling their chains maybe to the point of breaking.

And when I got to the top of the hill I ran fast to the car, opened the door, and rolled up the windows with the furious dogs just a few yards away. Deafened, I grabbed the key and started the car, and here came the shots from behind. Nélson, hot on my heels, the car already moving, I see Nélson in the rearview setting the dogs loose, drive the car at a foolish speed, jolting ahead without direction, can't find the dirt path, hit a stone, crash against another, the dogs appear, throwing themselves against the windows. I hear shots, Nélson's chasing behind them, definitely trying to shoot out the tires, I don't see Léo in the rearview, a huge rock in front of me, one of the dogs unleashing its fury between me and the rock, and I hit the gas and smash the dog against the rock, bashing the car two, three times against the rock, splattering blood on the windshield. Turn now to the left, a shot shatters the back window, finally hit the dirt road, floor it, going, going, dust, dust from all sides, I almost lose visibility, the car skidding off the dirt road, going, going anywhere, the crack of the shots more and more distant, the barking of the dogs sinking away, ten minutes later an absolute silence. I stopped the car.

A few yards in front of me, a barbed-wire fence. On the other side, not too far, an old bus rumbled down a road. I thought I might be safe for the time being. I was breathing with difficulty. Had an attack of hiccups. I opened the car door and walked ahead, looking behind, all around, no danger in sight.

I took my time getting between two of the wires on the fence. I ripped my pants on a low, nude branch. After stumbling over something, I fell. The sun was very strong. I had a hard time getting up. I took off my coat and threw it on the ground. Aside from making me sweat, it weighed too much. I threw it away without the least desire to turn back and look at it one last time.

It was a dirt road, not the same one that brought us to the farm. It reinforced the sensation I was being rescued from Nélson's clutches.

I saw a horse-drawn wagon approaching. The guy driving it was by himself. I waved and he stopped. I said I'd gotten lost. For two days I'd wandered, from dawn until dusk, without finding anybody. I didn't know how this could have happened to me.

"I need your help, I need you to give me a lift," I said.

"Sure, climb on up," he said.

He was a young man. He didn't seem at all perturbed by my sudden appearance in a state of emergency. Just told me to climb onto the wagon. Seated beside him on the wagon seat, I asked where he was heading.

"To Viçoso, at the foot of that hill over there," he responded.

I saw a low hill a few miles ahead. Houses, people, whatever he was calling Viçoso still remained to be seen.

"The hill, and what's after that?" The question came out too quickly.

"After that hill is where Rio Grande do Sul begins," he replied.

I looked at the horse's haunches as it marched, looked at the young man gone blond and wizened by the sun, looked back at the cargo he was carrying, squash. The wagon was shaking; I asked, "You taking those squash to Viçoso?"

"To sell in Viçoso. I live there."

"So you live almost at the border of Rio Grande," I remarked.

"At one time I lived in the north of Rio Grande."

"What did you do there?"

"I transported sand, wood, bricks, construction stuff."

I thought it would be nice if this journey lasted a while, that we wouldn't get to Viçoso until the end of the day, so that by the time we arrived there'd only be time to eat something, find a place to stay, and go to sleep.

In fact, we did arrive in the evening. The road was full of curves, skirting hills. Viçoso was a village with pretty much just one real street. The side streets didn't extend for more than four or five houses. Beyond those houses the soil eroded, cleaving into a furrowed ravine.

I went to the end of one of the side streets. To the right the orange sun was falling behind the hill. Before me was a tree whose branches were plucked by winter. The winter had turned the surrounding fields gray.

I was alone, staring at a countryside that looked like a plateau, when I heard the voice of the guy from the wagon just behind me.

"Sir, I arranged a place for you to sleep," he said.

I turned around and said, "Where?"

"In the parsonage," he replied.

"You spoke with the priest?" I asked.

"No, the priest only comes once a month—I

spoke with Antônio, the guy who lives in the house and takes care of the church. He said you could go there."

I said thanks, and asked, "And where can I find something to eat?"

"I'll take you to Big Paul's bar. He's a friend of mine."

We sat down in the bar. Big Paul was a redhead with very curly hair. On the table was a linen tablecloth, stained with egg on one edge. Men were drinking, some were seated at the tables, others were standing and leaning against the bar. The boy who'd brought me in the wagon rubbed his hands. Big Paul brought us some beer. Two men were discussing how awfully hot it was for July. I took off my old blazer, which I almost never did. I could smell my sweat, wondered how I'd wash my clothes. I didn't have anything to change into, and I was really starting to stink. Since the guy I came with didn't talk much, I was able, even while in his company, to mull over such details without feeling hemmed or pressured.

"I get the impression this is a really nice place," I remarked.

"I never made an enemy in Viçoso," he said.

"A nice place to stay," I ventured.

"Where are you from, sir?" he asked.

"I'm from Rio de Janeiro."

"From Rio?" he repeated.

"That's where I'm from."

"And where are you going after Viçoso?"

"I'll cross the border into Rio Grande, I'm heading that way," I replied, raising my arm as though about to point in that direction.

"Ah!…" the guy exclaimed.

Big Paul appeared with two steaks, rice, beans, lettuce. Outside it was already nighttime. Some men were gathered at the door to the bar. The extraordinary July heat remained the topic of conversation.

When we finished eating I felt tired; asked my guide to take me to the parsonage.

A woman opened the door to us. She was the housemaid. Antônio was seated, facing the door, but got up. I told him I was traveling, and that it was just a night's stay.

"Yes," Antônio said, "we have one empty bed,

one vacant room."

He opened the door to the room, and the first thing I saw was a bed covered with a white sheet, which draped down the sides.

A floorboard creaked as I entered. On the wall over the headboard was a crucifix. Antônio closed the door.

I took a few steps, so drunk with sleep that just before reaching the bed my legs gave out and I fell to my knees on the floor.

With my arms I found the bed.

My head was hanging. A drop of sweat was ready to fall from the tip of my nose.

When I woke in the morning I was still there, with my knees on the floor—my arms, chest, and head on the bed.

Once again I couldn't immediately recognize the place where I'd awakened. I didn't move my body, only turned my pupils upward and saw the crucifix against the white wall. I lifted my head and chest, smoothed the sheet.

This gesture of smoothing the sheet transmitted

a sensation of relaxation that had, for a while, been inaccessible.

It made me get up, go to the window, and lift the sash. The day was radiant, the temperature just like summer. I took off my shirt.

The window looked out onto a spacious patio. At the back, a white wall. Chickens were scratching beneath a lime tree. I leaned over the windowsill. The cleaning lady was stretching a white sheet across the clothesline.

I had an urge to call out to her but restrained myself—I didn't know her name.

In the distance I heard the hideous squeal of a pig that knew it was about to be slaughtered.

I rubbed my eyes: the light was intense. I looked at my watch.

It was necessary to face the day in some other way. But I didn't know how.

I opened the bedroom door. Antônio was coming out of the bathroom. The flush of the toilet was still audible. We exchanged a good morning. I said I needed to take a bath. Antônio said he'd give me a towel.

"There's always a clean bath towel here for anyone who stays over," he said.

"That's great," I said.

*Who is Antônio?* I wondered while I followed him to a room where he got me the towel.

"You can have coffee after," he said, passing me a white towel.

"There are so many white things here," I said, taking the towel.

Antônio smiled. And he asked if I needed my clothes washed. If I didn't have anything else to wear, he'd lend me the frock of a priest who'd died three years prior. It was Father Anselmo, who was eighty-seven when he died—his whole life assigned to Viçoso. The frock was totally worn through, all frayed at the edges, but it was just to wear while my clothes dried.

Antônio told me that aside from what he was wearing all he had were the shirt and pants Marisa had just put in the wash. So he couldn't lend me any clothes of his own.

"Since it's so sunny out, the clothes will be dry by early afternoon," he told me.

"Great," I said.

And I added, without much internal conviction, as always seemed to be the case when I referred to the course of my journey, "In early afternoon I'll be on my way."

I was drinking coffee with milk and eating a thick slice of buttered bread, in Father Anselmo's old frock. Antônio was sitting in the same chair I'd found him in when I arrived at the house. Only he had now turned the chair in my direction.

He told me he'd lived in Rome for four years. There he'd known hunger, absolute misery. He'd wandered the streets in rags. Eaten whatever he was given. Sometimes he sat on the doorstep of a fancy restaurant until a cop gave him the boot or a waiter brought him something to eat—the remains of the customers' meals, usually, heaped into a cardboard carton.

"I'd go into a corner and eat it with my hands.

"At the end of every summer I'd find a shelter run by one of the religious orders. And so one year I started making love to a nun. I had noticed she was devoted to me in a very special way. One time she smuggled me two chicken wings.

"Late one afternoon, as we passed each other in the shelter's hallway, she told me to follow her to the pantry so she could sneak me a jar of fig jam.

"We went into the pantry, and I closed the door behind us. She made like she was about to scream. I pushed her up against a shelf. Some cans fell. I lifted her habit. I pulled, ripped whatever she was wearing underneath. Since she was squeezing her legs shut, her thighs trembling, I took her by the shoulders and forced her onto the floor. I got on top of her, and it was easier that way. She wasn't resisting anymore. She just mumbled with a little moan when I penetrated her: 'My God!'"

The story was making me nervous. After all, I was wearing a soutane while he was telling me all this. I began to suspect I'd landed in some trouble: here I was dressed as a priest while Antônio had me picture him raping a nun.

As soon as my clothes were dry I'd leave. Maybe I'd be able to hitch a ride somewhere. Antônio was telling me how, after that, he was never left in peace.

"The nun started inviting me to the pantry every day, saying she had cookies, fruit, candy. I didn't even always feel like it. But since I was young, I just got right to it, fulfilled my duty in exchange for a few things, which at the time were delicacies to me."

I had my last sip of coffee and thought about taking a walk around Viçoso. Listening to the story about the ravenous nun while sitting in that frock had left me in a state of discomfort I hoped to dispel by walking around outside.

When I walked past Antônio, who was still sitting in his chair, I realized that he must have been a good-looking man. Now he was used-up like me, missing a tooth on one side.

The frock was too short for me. Since I'd even sent my socks to be washed, my shins were bare, exposed, dirty old shoes on my feet. I'd have to be careful in case a wind kicked up the frock, since my underwear was also in the laundry.

After opening the door to the street I saw a decent-sized part of a splintered tree trunk lying neglected on the stone sidewalk. I picked it up, and thought it would make a great walking stick.

I went out leaning on it, almost as if I were blind, because no one in Viçoso would come close to the frock or a blind man's staff—they'd leave a respectful aura around such a figure, so as not to disturb his solitary walk.

I went down the street with my eyes straight ahead, fixed. Every now and then I heard a "God Bless"—a greeting—I couldn't help but notice a little girl's timid gesture. I responded to nothing. I was an unknown figure with his staff; no one came very close.

Perhaps for some I was a man in constant touch with sacred spheres, who didn't see the visible world. I also couldn't help noticing an old woman with a demented expression get down on her knees as I passed.

When I got to Big Paul's bar I realized where I was. I shielded my face with my hand so no one would recognize me.

Walking past, I looked between my fingers and from the corner of my eye saw a guy leaning against the bar that looked to me like Léo. I shut my fingers, shielding my eyes with them, as though protecting myself from the sun.

And if it were Léo, would Nélson be with him, hunting me?

I didn't wait to find out, and kept moving, faster, but not so fast that anyone would get suspicious of anything. I took one of the side streets, thinking I'd slink along the edge of the village to get back to the parsonage.

I was almost at the end of the street, ready to hike up my frock and traipse down into the ravine that bordered Viçoso, when I heard a sob. I looked around and noticed that the last house on my right had its door open. That was where the sob had come from.

I went in. I saw a wrinkled old woman, crying. When she saw me she rushed over, saying God had sent me. She said her sister was dying in the bedroom, and God had sent me to give last rites to her sister, Diva.

The old woman took me to the bedroom by the hand. Her sister, Diva, looked even older, with dark blotches on her hands and face. She was moaning, and held a rosary in her hands.

I preferred not to give up my staff. I leaned over and waved my hand above her eyes, which were wide open. Her pupils didn't react. The old woman who had guided me to her sister's deathbed continued to cry. The moribund woman's labored breathing came and went in what seemed to be her final gasps. When she inhaled it was accompanied by a spasm in her jaw. She was no longer moaning.

"Father, it's time," said the old woman who'd brought me.

Instinctively I knew I was lacking sacred oil or whatever. I pressed my right thumb onto my tongue, felt it moisten, and made a cross with it on the forehead, the mouth, and the chest of the dying woman. And then I said softly, "Go, Diva, go without fear, go…"

Then the old woman gave a sigh and died.

I left the dead woman's house and went to the corner of the little side street and the main road. I surveilled the scene: there wasn't anyone in front of Big Paul's bar, everything seemed calm. I needed to be as careful as possible—it was the third death in my presence in just three or four days.

But performing the last rites had left me with a feeling of strength: yes, I'd walk back by way of the main street for all to see, without sneaking around the outskirts of Viçoso.

I resumed walking with my staff. The same gait as before: someone who can't be bothered with worldly things, someone who tolerates the blindness that opens him to contact with other forces. Interrupting me would have amounted to an insult.

This time there wasn't a single living soul at Big Paul's bar.

I went into the parsonage through the patio gate. I saw a woman stretching out another sheet. Fat, with big boobs, her wet skirt sticking to her thighs. I remembered her name, Marisa. I stopped in front of her and said, "Marisa, was it sunny enough for my clothes to dry?"

"Almost, they'll be dry in a little bit."

I could tell that we were more or less hidden between the hanging sheets. I threw down my staff. She stared at me, a basin full of suds tucked between her hip and arm. I moved forward and kissed her neck. I heard the basin fall, opened her blouse buttons, and kissed her breasts. I lifted the wet skirt and squeezed her thighs—she wasn't wearing underwear.

Marisa opened a few buttons on the frock and we both came standing up.

I entered the house through the kitchen. My crotch was wet. Antônio still sat in his usual chair. I pulled up a chair and sat down in front of him, and said, "Not a cloud in the sky, it's going to stay hot."

"You never asked me how I ended up here," he said to me.

"I listen. I listen to everything—I don't ask," I said.

I had an uneasy premonition as I said it. I wanted only silence before leaving this house. But here was Antônio, my host, and he wanted me to know his life story.

Antônio went on, navigating the high seas of the South Pacific, sailing to an island called Naia.

"What a long trek," I remarked.

He didn't hear me. Then I saw him shrink back

with a shudder, as if he'd been stabbed, twist in his seat, and fall, convulsing, to the floor. Drool ran out of his mouth. I called Marisa.

She came, and proceeded as though she were fulfilling a daily chore: she opened Antônio's shirt and waited, kneeling by his side, for the attack to cease.

Then, when the body calmed and returned to normal, she wiped a handkerchief across Antônio's mouth. And went back out to the patio.

Antônio got up by himself and sat in the old chair.

He had a tremendously lost look in his eyes, perhaps seeing the South Pacific. He didn't seem to register my presence.

From the kitchen door I asked Marisa if I could put my clothes back on yet. I said with a little laugh that I was getting cooked alive in the frock. She said, yes, my clothes were dry, she only needed to iron them.

I went out to the patio. On tiptoe, I plucked an orange. I went back to the kitchen, got a knife. I sat down on the step between the kitchen and the patio, and began to peel the orange. I ate the orange the same way I always did, cutting off hunks with the knife.

Marisa appeared with my ironed clothes. I stayed seated on the stoop. My socks and underwear were on top of my folded shirt and pants. The blazer was hanging from one of her hands. I said she'd been very fast. She didn't seem affected by the praise. She merely said she'd put my clothes on the bed where I'd slept. I craned my neck to watch as she walked away with such purpose that I only managed to see a flutter of her skirt disappearing down the hallway.

"It's time for me to leave," I murmured.

When I went into the bedroom I saw the clothes on top of the bed. I sat on the bed. *I need to decide*, I mused. Looked at the crucifix on the wall. Everything seemed to last for an infinity.

I closed the door and began taking off the frock. In two seconds I'd cast off the likeness of a priest. I was a man standing naked before a crucifix on a wall. I shivered.

I cupped my hand around my sex. Sticky. I wrapped myself in the sheet, walked quickly down the hall, went into the bathroom, and turned on the shower. I heard the grating sound of a sawmill.

When it was time to leave I went to say goodbye to Antônio. He was sitting in his eternal chair, in the same position as when I'd met him: legs crossed, staring at the door to the street. Only he didn't seem to see me now. Glassy eyes facing the door.

His skin after the attack, withered.

I bent down, took his hand and kissed it. I felt him tremble.

Into his ear I said only this, "Thank you."

And I withdrew.

When I went through the kitchen door there were some ducks at the foot of the doorway. At my appearance they squawked and left en masse. I saw Marisa between the hanging sheets. I felt a dart of passion. But I wanted to eat lunch on the road, and it was getting pretty late.

So I only gave her a soft kiss on the mouth and said I was leaving. She didn't seem bothered. I put some money in her hand, for the trouble of washing my clothes.

I opened the patio gate. A dog was barking at the heels of a horse going by. Mounted on the horse was a boy of about twelve, dressed as prince charming—a blue cape descended from his shoulders. There must be a school party, I guessed.

I stopped for a while in the shadow of a tree, huffing and puffing from the heat. I did this because I figured the residents of Viçoso would like someone who behaved so demonstratively.

Like this child on the porch of the cottage in front of me. Spinning, jumping, at times peering in one of the windows. Since almost no one else was passing along the streets of Viçoso, the girl took a moment to size me up, and she was smiling. I don't know if she was happy for some reason, all I know is she was smiling, and when she saw me she didn't stop, and her smile included me too, so I smiled as well.

And with that smile on my lips I began to walk once more.

As I left Viçoso, descending like a vagabond into the ravine that bordered the city, I heard thunder, a hollow sound coming from the line of the horizon, where I saw a very dark storm brewing, which made me wonder if I wasn't committing a blunder by confronting it.

I spat on the red earth. I got the feeling I was accepting a challenge. Then scraped my foot over the saliva.

When I next took note, the monumental mass of dark clouds was already looming overhead. I turned around, knowing I was looking at Viçoso for the last time. Everything I'd lived through in Viçoso flashed by in an instant, as if I needed to take a quick account of everything to feel like I was actually ready to leave.

Viçoso looked much different beneath the dark

mass—it was difficult to imagine Marisa underneath that sky. Antônio might not withstand the
weight of the clouds and might have died already.

I felt the first drops of rain on my skin. The
smell of wet earth took to the air.

With the rain came the cold—winter's return. Even
so, I kept walking away from Viçoso. Drenched, I
found a narrow path and went down it.

It gave the impression of a dark night having
fallen, so dark I couldn't read the time off my watch.
But by my calculations it couldn't have been past
mid-afternoon.

From time to time bright lightning flashed, al-
lowing me to see the immensity that lay ahead. It
was thundering. A bolt of lightning struck nearby
and rumbled in the earth—I cringed. In one of the
flashes I saw a nude tree beside some kind of shack.

I ran toward the little cottage, pushed against
the door—it creaked, opened. It was dark, with no
human noise. Cattle were lowing nearby. Toads
croaked ceaselessly.

As soon as I got inside I hunkered down to the

left of the door. I stayed there for a long time, calmly listening to the storm and hugging my body, which trembled from the cold.

I listened to the rain die down and then stop. My sight was restored by the returning light, which wasn't very bright, since it was already the end of the afternoon. I emerged from the shack and there was a full rainbow cutting across the dusky sky.

The atmosphere, now without a trace of wind, seemed crystallized by the cold, and was chilling me to the bone. Water was dripping from my entire body. My shaking intensified, and a deep cough set in; I decided to keep going.

It was already night when I saw some lights in the distance. It had been a long time since I'd hiked on dirt paths through open country or fallen into rain puddles. The terrain was now almost a swamp, and, with tremendous difficulty lifting my legs to take each step, I went toward those lights.

The lights grew larger, multiplied. As I drew near I saw it was a small city. There wasn't anybody on the streets, not a single car passing. Sidewalks wet, flooded in some places. A church steeple. A building that housed a newspaper called the *Arraiol Daily*. Someone was listening to an opera nearby.

I felt a pang in my chest. Then a coughing fit. For a moment my head reeled.

I knocked on a door. A woman wrapped in a quilt opened the door, looked me over—noticing I was all wet and covered with mud—and slammed the door with a scream. Then I heard her yell, "It's the kidnapper, help!"

I backed away from the house. Then I hastily turned around and saw in front of me the house from which the music emerged. I decided to give it another shot: I knocked on the door.

A fat, bald man opened the door. The record was turning out a nasal twang. The voice of a tenor. When the man took in my muddy state he pulled a gun from his pocket. And aimed at me.

Once more I backed away. Much more slowly this time, without twitching a finger. Now the voice was a soprano.

I thought it might be better to keep walking, at least to stay warm. From the end of the street a black and white Volkswagen police car approached, the red light on top spinning.

This spinning red light was the last thing I saw. I steadied myself on an iron gate and felt the strength drain out of me. I heard my head knock against the pavement.

When I opened my eyes the fat, bald man was beside me. Even with my foggy head, I could see he was smiling with delight.

There was a needle in my arm, which appeared to be injecting some kind of serum.

The bald guy came close to my ear and said he was the chief surgeon in Arraiol. His eighteen-year-old daughter had devoured celebrity magazines about soap stars since she was ten years old. She'd recognized me.

I tried to sit up, but my whole body hurt, and the surgeon's hands pressed me down.

Then he left. And then came a searing pain from my right leg. It felt like a lightning bolt tore through my body from my leg and lodged in my brain.

Before asking for an anesthetic, a sedative, I concentrated all my barely existent strength to lifting my head: they had amputated my right leg.

A black nurse appeared and stuck a needle in the vein of my free arm.

The next time I awoke there was a pretty girl beside me, holding my hand. She had a cold hand, a pale smile, and the look of someone who truly suffered. Blondish, with green eyes.

She told me she was the surgeon's daughter. She'd recognized me during one of her customary visits to the hospital, and all of Arraiol was rooting for me, praying for my rehabilitation.

"They amputated my right leg," I said.

She told me it was a last resort. Her father had had to do it.

Suddenly I felt the spark of a hope that all this might just be a nightmare. I got the familiar feeling that somebody was merely acting, in this case the girl. So, to then banish all doubt, I marshaled all possible energy, and thrust what should have been my right leg.

It didn't hurt as much now, but I had the clear sensation of only moving a short stump. The rest of the leg—the part that had existed below the stump—had preceded me in death. I raised my head and saw what I would continue seeing for the rest of my life: I was missing my right leg.

The end of the stump was bandaged.

I couldn't prevent tears from springing to my eyes, and the surgeon's daughter called out for Sebastião, the black nurse, so he could quickly sedate me, because I shouldn't suffer any additional distress.

The next time I woke, the nurse was close by, watching me. He gave me back my wallet. I'd forgotten all about it. Inside there was some money and my ID. Everything was still a bit wet from the storm I'd been caught in before arriving at this place they call Arraiol. I had only a vague recollection of the storm. The nurse said that, in a few days, my wallet and everything inside it would be dry.

After that he told me Dr. Carlos—the doctor who had performed my surgery, father of the girl

Diana whom I'd met—had stayed close by to observe me until recently.

The nurse also told me about an interview Dr. Carlos had given to a newspaper in Arraiol; all about the good press he'd gotten off my case. The procedure—this was how they referred to the amputation—had been the right decision. I'd soon be back in front of the TV cameras.

"To play the part of Saci Pererê," I said, in the flat tone I used whenever I tried to be funny.

"I have to admit that I didn't recognize you from TV," the nurse said.

"I did a few roles on soap operas, but that was back then I was a good-looking guy whose likeness graced the covers of magazines."

The nurse said he'd give me a bath now. My only clothing was a rather long piece of linen, tied in three places in the back. He asked me to roll to one side so he could untie it.

He undressed me very carefully and started to run a soapy sponge over my body.

During my bath I saw my uncovered stump for the first time. It was still deep purple, a huge wound on the end. It occurred to me that I'd better say something to try and forget the sudden nausea, "I think I heard Diana call you Sebastião," I recalled.

"My name is Sebastião," he confirmed, passing the sponge across my belly.

Then he wiped a warm cloth over my body to remove any remaining suds. He was saying it was Sunday, and that afternoon there'd be a game on TV. It was a friendly game, Brazil against Argentina, in Buenos Aires.

"Where are we? Where exactly is Arraiol?" I remembered to ask.

"Ah, my friend, still a bit of amnesia?" he said, smiling.

"Where are we?" I insisted, a bit impatiently.

"Don't tell me that you don't know that Arraiol is in Rio Grande do Sul, Brazil," he said, pretending to scold me, infantilizing me in that way of people who treat the gravely ill.

I stared at him. I focused my attention on the contrast between his very dark skin and his very white nurse's uniform.

"Are you from Arraiol?" I asked.

"I'm from a village far from here, called Sobroso. You?" he asked.

"I was born in Porto Alegre and lived there until my twenties."

"Do you go to Porto Alegre much?"

"I've never been back."

"You don't know anyone there anymore?"

"No," I replied.

Then Sebastião told a joke to cheer me up. The main character in the joke was a Danish woman in a dentist's chair. He ended the joke by letting out a raucous laugh.

I laughed. I noticed that the force of my laughter didn't hurt too much.

"Tomorrow I want to get up, sit in a chair," I said.

"The man in charge around here is Dr. Carlos. He makes all the decisions," Sebastião said.

Sebastião spoke in a way that made it clear he didn't like Dr. Carlos one bit.

I was sleeping less now—the intervals between one nap and the next much longer. At first I wasn't pleased that my sleep ratio—as Dr. Carlos called it—was decreasing.

The enhanced wakefulness left me fearful. As though I'd completely lost confidence in any other use of time but sleep.

I could still look around, and that's how I managed to pass the time I remained awake: I saw the Sacred Heart of Jesus in front of me; I saw the appearances of the people who came to look at the legless actor; I saw Dr. Carlos's bright bald head. And at times I regretted that, in addition to my leg, I hadn't also lost my sight.

Sebastião woke me one morning, saying the day had come for me to try to get around a bit in a wheelchair.

"Today we're going to get out of that bed," he repeated several times.

I drank coffee with milk and refused to eat anything, excited by the idea of getting out of bed for a while, seeing new things beyond that room. Besides that, I was getting sores on my back from spending so much time in bed.

Sebastião told me Diana would be coming soon. They'd given him the order to give me a special bath.

Then he gave me a sponge bath, and, for the first time, dusted me with talcum powder from my head to my only foot: my genitals, my behind, my back, my armpits. Dressed me in a pair of pajamas. Gray pajamas with wine-colored trim on the collar and cuffs.

Diana arrived a little after nine—in a green knit dress buttoned up the front. She smiled at me. Kissed me on the lips and gave a sigh. I took her hand, which was still as cold as the first time I touched it. Sebastião came into the room pushing a wheelchair.

He picked me up, one arm as my seat and the other arm as my backrest, and sat me in the wheelchair. During this entire procedure Diana was close, holding my hand.

She kissed my hand and started to push the wheelchair toward the corridor. It was a long corridor: some convalescents were wandering down it, steadying themselves on the walls.

From behind me, Diana was speaking softly

and slowly, as if trying to hold my attention. Telling me it was a special day for her father—the launch of his campaign for mayor of Arraiol. It was the first election in Arraiol. The town had just been incorporated a few months prior.

"My father fought the hardest for Arraiol's autonomy," she confided in my ear.

Out in the street, fireworks had begun to go off. Diana said—still pushing me along the corridor—that Dr. Carlos's motorcade, as they called it, was on its way. Of course it was going to pass by the hospital, and we'd watch the motorcade from the hospital balcony.

When we got to the balcony Diana straightened the blanket over my leg. Down below, a band was passing. Diana told me it was one of *Rigoletto*'s arias put to marching time—her father's favorite opera.

Diana was now telling me her father's candidacy was a coalition of three parties. The name of the coalition, written on a number of banners, was the Municipal Alliance. Wherever the name Municipal Alliance was written, the name of their candidate—Dr. Carlos—also appeared. Never with his last name. Diana made sure to tell me her father was known that way across the whole region. Nobody called him by his last name.

I discerned the figure of Dr. Carlos round the corner, approaching on the back of a truck, waving to the people standing on the curb.

Suddenly a guy with the name of the newspaper—*Arraiol Daily*—on his chest scaled the hospital wall and snapped a photo of me with Diana on the balcony. Then Diana grabbed my hand, just as the guy snapped another photo.

When Dr. Carlos passed in front of the hospital, he gave us a lingering wave. Diana waved back emotionally. People were either looking at him or at Diana and me. They clapped for us.

"It's the soap opera actor whose life the future mayor saved," I murmured, knowing I must look completely foolish.

"What's that?" Diana leaned down to ask, clapping continuously.

"I'll tell you later," I said, almost yelling over the loudspeakers.

After the motorcade went by, Diana took me through the hospital corridors. We didn't speak to each other. I heard only her panting.

"Would you like to see the hospital chapel?" she asked.

"Diana, Diana, anything you want," I replied.

The chapel was in the hospital courtyard. A ramp led up to the chapel door. Diana pushed the wheelchair harder to make it up the ramp. The door was closed. Diana pulled her dress away from her chest, and drew a key from inside.

"I have the key," she said.

And she opened the chapel door. She took me through the door, then closed it and turned the key.

She pushed my wheelchair up to the last row of pews in the chapel. Leaning down, she embraced me.

I asked her to open the buttons of her dress. I touched one of her breasts. It was so small that it fit almost entirely in my mouth.

She pulled out the other breast, told me I could do that one too. This breast tasted a little bit sweeter.

I put my hand on the crotch of my pajamas: I could tell I only had a partial erection.

Seated in the wheelchair, I could look out the window of my hospital room and see springtime arriving early. Flowers were already blossoming at the tops of trees.

I'd never taken off the gray pajamas. They now had faint stains only I noticed.

They'd given me wooden crutches, the kind that go underneath each arm, cushioned at the top. With the crutches I could sometimes wander around the room, but not farther.

Dr. Carlos hadn't come to check on me for about two weeks. He sent orders through Sebastião: I should do such and such exercises with my leg; I should try to walk so many minutes on my crutches down the corridor outside the room; I should drink less fluids.

Sebastião confided to me that he was going to leave the hospital to look for work as a nurse in another city.

"Very far from Arraiol, if possible. So far that I never hear any news from here."

"Take me with you," I said, laughing.

"You'll end up married to Dr. Carlos's only heiress," he said, letting out a laugh that was suddenly interrupted by a thought that silenced him.

Sometimes he'd take me for a stroll around the hospital courtyard. I liked the firm way he drove my wheelchair.

I still hadn't gone outside the hospital. One afternoon he insisted I make it all the way to the courtyard on crutches.

Under the open sky and without the wheelchair, I'd hardly crossed the threshold into the courtyard— the last step I'd taken with Sebasião's help—before I made a fool of myself. I lost my balance and fell into a bed of chrysanthemums.

At that time of day the courtyard was empty, so nobody besides Sebastião witnessed my fall. He pulled me out of the flowerbed and let me rest on the ground for a while, propped against a tree. He asked my forgiveness. I said I'd need to get used to falling from now on.

Then he picked me up and sat me on a low wall at the edge of a little pond in the middle of the courtyard.

There was a fountain in the pond. Little red fish swam around. A hunk of bread bobbed in the water. I felt a droplet hit my forehead.

"I'm going to call Diana," I said.

I thought calling would prevent me from becoming too despondent over my fall. The person who answered the phone was Dr. Carlos.

"How are you doing?" he asked.

"Better, Dr. Carlos."

"Yeah?"

"Yes, Dr. Carlos, I'd like to speak with Diana, please."

When Diana came to the phone she said, "My love, I dreamed of you all night."

"Then come and see me."

"On my way," she responded, breathless.

Except for these moments with Diana, or my conversations with Sebastião, the hours dragged on— nothing I got my hands on was worth reading. One day it was a book on the life of Saint Francis of Assisi. It started with him already a saint. It didn't say anything about his childhood, his youth, how he'd arrived at saintliness. The book began with Francisco already haloed.

I asked Sebastião to get rid of it.

He told me the hospital was like that, books just found their way to the patients, and a lot of times even to the hospital staff, without anybody knowing where they'd come from or why they ended up in certain hands and not others.

"You were sent *The Life of Francisco*. Can you guess who sent it?"

"Dr. Carlos?" I asked.

Sebastião stared at me without saying anything, his gaze completely absorbed.

"Okay, Sebastião, I already asked once, but please take me with you when you leave this place!"

"What did you say?" he asked.

"I said all this is bullshit."

"That's right, so we'll plan our escape," he said.

The fall I suffered in the hospital courtyard put me in a bad funk. I didn't want to walk on crutches anymore. For most of each day I only wanted to be in bed, hesitating even before agreeing to the wheelchair.

Even in the wheelchair, I didn't want to go to the courtyard anymore. I felt even more disabled under the open sky.

In the days after the fall I realized the only thing I was in the mood for was talking to Sebastião. Even Diana—always ready to offer me her firm breasts—wore me out as much as anything else. She was always going on about her father's greatness—the man who had taken away my leg.

At certain times, especially when Sebastião wasn't nearby, I calculated that the right time for going insane had arrived. I reflected: suppose the psychiatrist perceived I was feigning madness, he'd still end up sending me to an asylum, because to him feigning madness would be a sure sign of insanity.

When Sebastião reappeared, my desire to escape at all costs relaxed a little. I'd made it a habit to give whatever he said my full attention—something rare for me, as I'd always had trouble following people.

What Sebastião would say was exactly what I needed to hear to keep clinging to the meager life surrounding me.

Sebastião would sometimes relate mystic scenes so vividly that I didn't have to imagine anything, only listen to him.

One day he came into the room saying he'd seen a ghost. He told me this with the utmost composure—he'd seen something moving in the middle of a bush, oval-shaped, bright and luminous, radiating great protection.

Sebastião finished the story as he gave me an injection. He said I'd feel sleepy, and to give in to it.

"Give in to it," was the last thing I heard. And I slept wonderfully, one of those slumbers that destroys all traces of fatigue.

That's what kind of sleep it was, and when I came to the surface, the first thing I saw was rain against the windowpane. I felt sluggish, without any motivation, and if I could have done anything, it would have been to ask Sebastião to put me back to sleep.

Sebastião wasn't in the room. The rain beat against the glass, and it was that rain and that glass I watched when my eyes refused to close again.

I was awakened by Sebastião.

"How's it going, buddy, should we have dinner?"

"Sebastião, take me with you," I demanded sleepily.

"I'll take you, but wake up first, eat a little, and later we'll discuss our escape."

Sebastião carried me to a little table that stood to the left of the window. He sat me in a chair next to the table. On the table was a bowl of soup and a spoon, as well as a glass of water. I looked out the window and saw night was falling. It did me good to see that the day was ending and that I hadn't participated in it whatsoever. With this absence I felt myself getting even with the day.

The soup was chalky and pasty. I looked back to see if Sebastião was still in the room. No, he'd left.

The rain had let up somewhat—the streetlight outside could be seen clearly now. When I put another spoonful of soup in my mouth I felt that it was already cold. I'd gotten distracted, had forgotten to keep eating my soup. That's what Sebastião said: "You forgot there was a plate in front of you again."

"Yeah…" I said, staring at my plate with my head down.

"Is there so much to think about?" Sebastião asked.

"You know, Sebastião, if I make an effort I'm also capable of seeing a ghost."

"Ghost or no ghost, you have to eat every day, my friend!"

"Nothing changes?" I asked.

"Nope," Sebastião replied.

A bubble formed in my right nostril and immediately popped. My head was hanging, as if it were heavy.

Sebastião wiped my nose with a piece of toilet paper. He asked me to try to keep my head upright. For now I shouldn't go back to sleep.

Sebastião was stretching sheets over my bed. He asked if they were changing my linens regularly. I said I didn't recall, but I'd make an effort to remember.

"The question is: has the hospital changed your bedsheets or not?" Sebastião said, snapping his fingers close to me so I'd pay attention to what he was saying.

"Why, Sebastião?"

"Because your sheets aren't clean, just look!"

He showed me a yellow stain, urine, which left me totally humiliated. I lowered my eyes, and said sincerely, "Look at what I've come to."

Sebastião agreed that it was troubling that things had come to this—to the point of staining my clothes and pissing my sheets.

I laughed heartily. I thought Sebastião had great power over me. Turning everything into a joke, he was the person who traversed each day with me in that room.

If it rained, or was sunny, if it was springtime and nightfall was starting to come later—everything out the window was worthy of comment.

I was no longer intrigued by Dr. Carlos's prolonged absences. Let him stay away—I'd have time to make plans.

I hadn't decided anything about my future life, where I'd go, if I'd return to Rio or not. Everything was complicated now, very much so: I was mutilated.

One afternoon Diana turned up in my room. In a rather seasonal spring dress, yellow, two or three frills. She came close and said she wanted me to take her virginity today. We should go to the chapel—the safest place, according to her.

I was honest with Diana, and informed her that she'd be better off not waiting for me to recover from this phase. I was still very weak. But she'd caught me on a day I felt like trying at least. She kissed me right in my ear.

In the chapel we spent a while trying to situate ourselves on the seat of a pew. Finally, we got into the tried and true position—she on her back with me on top, everything open just right for me to get inside.

I could tell later, however, that I was like a lead weight on Diana, because that position, I didn't understand why, left me in a state of prostration from the stomach on down. Diana's body had turned into a sort of receptacle for the weight of my mutilated carcass. She was moaning because she couldn't breathe. Desperate, she pushed me onto the floor.

She left me alone in the chapel.

With considerable effort I managed to get up on the pew. Then I laid down on the seat and fell asleep, exhausted.

When I woke it was nighttime, everything dark. I saw a stained glass of the Resurrection lit by the moon. It didn't take me long to discover where I was.

I sat up on the chapel pew trying to feel my way. I couldn't see anything. Up front there was a little lantern. The flame trembled.

In the dark I had a hard time with the wheelchair, but managed to get it all the way to the door of the chapel, which wasn't locked.

There wasn't anybody in the courtyard. It was a cold night. When I opened the door to my room and turned on the light I saw Sebastião sleeping in my bed.

I turned out the light and went to the window in the wheelchair. The glass was all fogged up. I wrote my name on the glass with my finger.

I opened my eyes, lifted my head, and faced the window, which displayed a beautiful morning. I was still in the wheelchair.

There was a banner on the other side of the street that said VOTE FOR DR. CARLOS.

I supposed it was Sunday, because a bunch of kids were in the street holding pennants suggesting they were there for Dr. Carlos's big rally, which was scheduled to take place at 10:00 a.m. on Sunday.

Without a doubt, it was that very Sunday, because I could already hear the first chords of the marching band.

Sebastião yawned behind me. When I turned to look he was rousing himself.

"Good morning," he said.

"Good morning," I replied.

He sat up in bed. I asked if he could hear the marching band from Dr. Carlos's motorcade.

He looked back at me, scowling.

Then I asked him to give me something that would put me to sleep.

He got up and said he'd bring an injection.

While he shot the injection into my vein he told me he'd already asked to be relieved at the hospital. He had some savings and would use them to try to get work as a nurse in another city.

"Take me," I demanded, starting to fall into a profound sleep.

"I'll take you, my friend. I already said I'd take you…" As he spoke his voice was drifting, drifting away, and I wondered if I was dying, if this could be the end.

But a second before Sebastião's voice had fled and everything went dark, I had a slight shock, an unexpected spark of consciousness. I don't know what it was that nearly had the power to bring me back.

It was like cresting on a wave, then toppling under.

When I woke it was night—the light in the room was off, but I could see Sebastião's white uniform sitting near me.

"I gave you a bath," he said, "because I gave you such a big dose of sedative this morning—you were almost a goner."

"I have the impression that I remember almost dying," I murmured.

Sebastião sat at my side, holding me by the

hand. He said he'd take me with him. We'd be on the highway with spring in bloom.

"Right, Sebastião. Bring me a glass of water, my mouth is dry."

He brought me a glass of water. And he told me that, just after I fell asleep, before he realized he'd given me an excessive dose, he'd deflowered Dr. Carlos's daughter.

"She came in the room right after you fell asleep. She started telling me there was a strange patient in the chapel. He was refusing to leave. When she took the key out of her dress, I figured: well here's another hot blonde coming around wanting to get fucked by a big black guy. Only I didn't expect her to be a virgin."

I told Sebastião I'd only sucked her breasts, things didn't go any further than that.

Sebastião turned on the light. He straightened my blanket, said his shift was starting; it promised to be a busy night. And he left.

I woke the next morning to Dr. Carlos pressing on the stump I now had instead of a leg.

There were some young residents around him. One of them asked how this would affect my bone structure.

Dr. Carlos responded: "We live in a world of structures. As in any other, when one part is removed from the skeleton, the whole structure is affected."

The students took notes on his words. Only one young man never pulled out a pen. He gazed at me, transfixed. He seemed to need a sign from me so he could come tell me something that for him, in that moment, was almost life itself. He didn't stop staring, and didn't disguise it.

Dr. Carlos said that was it for today, they could go—they'd see each other again on Thursday. Only then did the young man lower his gaze. He left the room with his colleagues.

As soon as the residents withdrew, Dr. Carlos began to enumerate a bunch of different walks I should do on my crutches, as well as some other exercises, because my release from the hospital was approaching.

*Where will I go?* I thought. And Sebastião…was he serious when he said he'd take me with him?

And Dr. Carlos, with his indifferent air, was clearly realizing that my reputation—despite the fame I still had among strange girls like his daughter—had been a flash in the pan, and my washed-up career didn't energize the sort of voters he needed.

Since I could tell that my life at the hospital was reaching an end, I began to exercise daily on my crutches. I went to the courtyard, sat on a bench near the chapel.

I made friends with a reddish dog. A short-haired mutt that immediately fell in love with me. I'd walk along the courtyard, and he'd come along at my side or sometimes behind me, always at the same pace, never hurried. Occasionally, when I lagged behind, he would stop, turn to me, his tail wagging, and wait.

When I sat on the bench, he'd lie down next to my foot. I was thinking of ways to take the dog when I left the hospital. People in my situation, with incomplete bodies, they need a dog.

One afternoon I heard someone playing the organ in the chapel. I later found out it was a young guy who'd been studying government in Germany. He'd learned he had a terminal cancer and came to die in Arraiol, his native land.

I stayed. Seated on a bench in the courtyard, listening to the organ with the dog against my foot. I stared at my missing leg, massaging the stump as though I still couldn't believe it, and watched a couple of convalescents walking with difficulties like mine. I found the world rather sad. Sometimes Sebastião waved to me from the door that led out to the courtyard. I waved back, the red dog curling snugly around my foot.

Such were my walks outside the hospital building. When I got up the dog would follow me. He wasn't too bold a creature, never daring to cross the threshold into the building.

They put me in a ward with a whole bunch of invalids. When I went to the ward I had to traverse a long aisle between the beds, hearing moans as I passed, cavernous breathing, sometimes delirium.

My bed was the last one—it took a few minutes to cross the ward all the way to the very end. As I went by, some of the invalids greeted me. Two or three seemed eager for conversation.

I'd lean my crutches against the wall and lie down, feeling tired out by so many short steps.

Sebastião was still my nurse, but he couldn't stay with me for very long. In a ward with so many invalids, he couldn't devote himself to just one.

Our conversations had more of an objective now: we were seriously planning to leave Arraiol together. Sebastião had a car. Trusting blindly in him, I believed that he carried me in his heart, that I'd be able to be useful to him in some way.

He had just fifteen more days to work at the hospital. It was more or less the period Dr. Carlos had estimated before I was to be released. Things were coinciding, and the two of us had to muffle our laughter on the ward. Usually Sebastião was the first to remember that we'd better quiet down.

"A few days from now, out there, we can laugh until we explode," he'd tell me.

The night before the date we'd selected, I left all my clothes in order on top of my nightstand. I remembered to fold the right pant leg a few times and fasten it with two safety pins. I didn't understand the utility of those folds, but it's what I'd seen other stumped men do.

The next day I woke as day was breaking. I dressed myself unhurriedly. A songbird was singing deep notes nearby.

Even with their rubber tips the crutches made a repetitive noise on the sidewalk.

Three blocks from the hospital I found Sebastião's rather old blue Volkswagen. Everything like we planned: that corner, out of view of the hospital.

When he saw me he gave a little toot on the horn. He got out of the car and opened the door for me. I wedged the crutches at a crooked angle between the floor and the back seat. They didn't really fit in a VW.

As I closed the car door I saw the red-haired dog looking at me from the other side of the street. I opened the window and made like I was going to stick my head out, say something, give him a signal. But I couldn't think of anything to save that friendship.

And the dog was already heading back, slowly, sure to resume his post in the hospital courtyard.

Sebastião got into the car, scratched his head and said, "I think it would be great if we went to Porto Alegre."

"I don't know anybody there anymore," I said.

"I know, you already told me, but my grand-mother lives there and I've been meaning to see her for ages," he said.

"Porto Alegre…" I said, "It's been years since I've been back."

"So then let's go?" Sebastião sighed.

"Of course, Sebastião, let's take advantage of this lovely morning for a road trip."

We stopped at a gas station as we were leaving Arraiol. There was a line of three or four cars. While we waited, I remarked that I didn't want to think about what I'd do when my money ran out.

In no time at all, after crossing out of Arraiol, the car was on a highway that cut through the hills, each one greener than the next. Sebastião was whistling.

"Look at that flock of sheep over there," he pointed.

On some stretches, the sides of the highway bloomed with flowers, mostly daisies. Sebastião told me he liked driving on the highway.

It was after noon when we stopped for the first time, in front of a restaurant on the side of the road. The restaurant was behind a gas station. When we got out of the car the smell of oil was hanging in the air.

The entrance to the bathroom was outside the restaurant. We both made for it, Sebastião shortening his gait the way people do when they accompany a cripple.

We pissed standing next to each other. Sebastião took one of the crutches. With my free hand I leaned against the wall. As I urinated I thought about what a chore this would be from now on.

But on that morning of my liberation from Dr. Carlos's empire, everything seemed less heavy— even the worst things were providential signs.

Sebastião ordered Cornish hen with polenta. I had chicken soup. It was the first time since losing my leg that I'd had any appetite for a meal. I slopped some broth onto the saucer and glanced at Sebastião. He was looking at me with admiration.

"We'll get to Porto Alegre around four in the afternoon," he said.

"That's a good time," I responded, returning to my bowl of soup.

As we were leaving the restaurant I noticed that Sebastião sometimes grew distracted and got ahead of me, then realized it, stopped, and turned to say something, like: "I think the trip will go quickly from here on. The weather's nice."

To get to the car we needed to pass the gas pumps and through the strong stench of oil. On the ground I saw some forgotten metal object, with fibrous pieces, which seemed like the thing most affected by the gas station's oil. The object was blacker than black, and whatever its prior function had been, it was now a thing like my amputated leg: lost forever.

Sebastião opened the door for me from inside

the car. When I sat down I noticed he'd switched on the radio, low volume, barely audible. The car got on the highway.

Sometimes a heavy truck was in front of us for a while, getting in our way. After passing it, if he could, Sebastião would look over at me, as if he'd just pulled off a remarkable feat.

"I just got the car—I could only afford to buy it recently," he told me.

Suddenly I felt very tired. Sebastião stopped on the shoulder to help me move to the back seat so I could sleep more comfortably. The crutches were standing almost upright, propped in the front against the seat.

I curled up and lay down. Sebastião turned off the radio and continued down the highway.

I slept. I had a strange dream in which I was a woman again. Only now, in accord with my waking life, I was a woman who was missing a leg. I, this woman, was at a train station in the hinterlands— nothing around but forest—waiting for someone I wasn't sure I'd see. Then the train arrived, filling the surroundings with smoke, and I couldn't see anything.… Then I woke up.

I stayed lying down, without saying anything. For a long time afterward, Sebastião thought I was still sleeping. Then, at some point, he said my name softly.

"Hey, I'm awake," I said.

He gave a glance back and said that, just like we'd thought, we'd get to Porto Alegre around four.

We were entering Porto Alegre. Sebastião was telling me how, until he was twenty years old, he spent a month out of every year with this grandmother in Porto Alegre. He liked her a lot. She lived in the Mont'Serrat neighborhood.

When we got to the address Sebastião had on a yellowed slip of paper, we saw there was no longer the blue wooden house he now described to me down to the most minute detail, with the hope that I'd help him find it.

Now, in its place, they'd erected a four-story building—visibly new construction. I asked if he was in touch with his grandmother. He said no, he hadn't seen her since he was twenty years old, and they didn't write each other because she was illiterate.

"The old lady told me once that she didn't have any close friends in Porto Alegre who could read or write for her. She worked for many years as a hotel maid, but she was very private, kept her words to herself, and few people understood what she said. When she wasn't cleaning she folded her arms against her chest, hiding herself. Her closest friends, she used to tell me, jokingly, were even more illiterate than she was. With me, though, she was a different person, she even laughed."

Then Sebastião looked ahead, asked if I could see that corner store. His grandmother had sometimes bought things there, they might know something about her.

I stayed in the car, looking in every direction, admiring the steep inclines of the neighborhood. The car was parked at a low point, and straight ahead was a hill so steep I couldn't see the top. I opened the window beside me.

Sebastião didn't take long in the corner store. He came, leaned into my window, and said it was the same old owner at the corner store. He'd given him the news that his grandmother had died a little more than two years ago, and the owner of the house had sold the property to the developers of the new building.

Sebastião moved back from the car a little, looked at the sky, said the weather was still nice.

"Oh, the sea," he exclaimed suddenly, "I've still never seen it!"

"You've never seen the sea?" I asked.

"Not yet," he replied.

"Look, Sebastião," I said, "we'll take the highway to Pinhal; it's the beach I used to go to when I was a kid."

Between Porto Alegre and Viamão we stopped at a café, both of us thirsty. There was a bar, and we leaned against it drinking mineral water. The man working the counter said it was already getting into the hot part of the year, but the cold had been stubborn this year.

Through the vents in front of us I noticed the light outside was failing. Sebastião was having an animated conversation with the bartender, telling him he was going to see the sea for the first time.

"No way," said the man across the counter.

"For the first time," Sebastião repeated.

Then we went back to the car. We didn't stop again until we got to Pinhal, an hour or so later.

Night had already fallen. There wasn't anybody on the streets. The car passed several summer cottages, all of them shuttered.

"Ghost town," Sebastião said, pretending to be scared.

We found a hotel. It was called the Atlantic. The letters were peeling from its white walls. Right in front of the hotel was a lamppost. A fine mist was visible against the light.

The woman who greeted us said she and her husband had started operating the hotel only recently. They were still getting things organized, but the rooms were cleaned every morning, and her husband, who was the cook, was already making the daily meals.

She was talking to us in the hotel restaurant itself. A spacious dining room with many tables, full of windows to the street. All the walls were peeling.

At the back of the room was an opening in the wall, with an arch at the top, which looked into the kitchen. The woman went over to the opening to call her husband, who was stirring something in a huge pot with a big metal spoon. She had told us her husband practically never came out of the kitchen—he liked being there more than being out in the hotel—and she was the one who served the food.

She introduced us to her husband and choked slightly as she said, "Look, our new guests."

Sebastião asked the man, who was rather tall and needed to duck to see us from the other side of the opening, how the hotel business was going. The man replied that the hotels along the coast had a lot of guests on spring weekends in other years. This year, with the cold lasting longer, there was almost nobody coming to stay.

"And the crisis, too," the woman reminded us.

The rooms were in another building, about twenty yards from the restaurant. As we crossed the grounds between one building and the other, I caught the soft fragrance of flowers. A dog was barking nearby—I couldn't see him, but he was close and it made me feel unsafe. The woman said the dogs around there didn't attack anybody—they only knew how to bark. Sebastião was leading the way, and now it was the woman who managed the hotel that hung back, half looking behind her to keep with my slow pace.

I stopped for a second, looked up, and saw a full moon, faint from the mist. Then I lowered my eyes and saw a stack of logs. I asked why all the logs. She told me they were firewood—her husband cooked on a big woodstove.

Sebastião wasn't carrying much luggage. Just one suitcase, which he now placed on the bed that would be his. The owner of the hotel said we would be the only two guests. If we wanted to call her or ask for something it was just a matter of whistling—it wouldn't bother anybody. Before closing the door to the room—which looked directly onto the street—she told us we were two blocks from the sea.

I'd sat down in a chair beside a small desk. Took off my blazer; not because I was hot, but just for the simple pleasure of tossing it onto the bed where I'd be sleeping, like I was at home. And I really felt at home for the first time, after so long.

Sitting on his bed, Sebastião was taking off his shoes.

I took off my shoe and saw my foot was rather swollen. I ran a hand over my head, hoping to ward off any bad thoughts that might occur about the remaining foot.

I leaned on the desk, got up, and made it to the bed in three hops. Lay down. Sebastião reminded me not to fall asleep—we'd have dinner first.

We heard the sound of someone chopping wood. We tried to guess which one of them would be cutting the wood, if it was him or her.

*We have so much time to guess so many things*, I thought, grabbed the pillow, and threw it up in the air. The chopping noise had already stopped.

"And the sea?" I asked.

"I want to see it tomorrow, in the daytime," he said.

"Did you realize we can hear it from here?" I asked.

"That's it?" he said, a finger in the air.

"That's it, Sebastião."

After dinner, the manager of the hotel, appearing for the first time outside of the kitchen, brought us two bowls of corn pudding. He liked to smile more than he liked to talk. I looked at my watch—it was nine in the evening.

I told Sebastião I was getting tired. He said he was, too. He told me he'd stolen some syringes and a few vials of sedative from the hospital in case I had trouble sleeping.

Sebastião said goodnight and turned out the light. I wondered what would become of me if Sebastião were to disappear. The beds were close enough for me to catch his scent. I listened as he began to breathe deeply.

"Sebastião," I called out. I asked him to give me an injection to sleep.

Sebastião asked me to sit up as he held up the

vial and shook it in the light.

I fumbled a bit from fatigue as I tried to prop myself against the wall. Sebastião lifted me by the underarms to help.

When he pulled the needle from my arm I was staring straight ahead, coveting the smoothness of the blue wall, without a single picture on it, without anything on it at all.

The injection was strong, I could tell. It wasn't long before I lay down again—I didn't want sleep to overtake me in an awkward position. I curled up in the way I like to sleep, said to Sebastião that one day I hoped I would understand why all this had happened.

The next morning when we woke, Sebastião told me that I'd stayed awake talking for a long time, resisting sleep, my voice coming out syrupy, and finally just babbling.

"What was I saying?" I asked.

"As far as I could understand, you were going to go back for a blue shirt."

Sebastião got up, then opened a window to let

in the sun. It was still early, a rooster crowing. From the bed I could see two hens on top of the woodpile.

Sebastião took a shower.

I stretched out sharply. The bed swayed and knocked over the crutches I'd left leaning against the wall next to the bed.

From the bathroom, Sebastião asked what had happened. I told him the crutches had slid down the wall.

"Ah," he replied.

And he started to sing a song I'd never heard before.

It sounded like music from the country. Slow, and the words spoke of longing for home.

Sebastião had a nice voice. It made me want to get out of bed with my single leg, go over to the door of the bathroom, and watch him. I had the sensation he was the last person I'd ever see.

When I managed to make it to the bathroom, after going through the complicated maneuvers I used when I wasn't on crutches, I saw Sebastião shaving.

I watched Sebastião. He was shaving and saw

me in the mirror. It looked like he was wearing new clothes—khakis and a green shirt.

"How's it going, my friend?" he said to me in the mirror.

"Sebastião…" I said.

"It's a great day for me to see the sea for the first time, did you look outside?" he asked, drying his face with a towel.

"Like the first day of creation," I replied.

That was when I began sliding down the door frame, without being able to stop myself. All my remaining strength was crumbling, like when a building implodes—that was how I was falling, and as I was collapsing the first thing I noticed was that I was losing my hearing—and by the time my body shattered against the slab floor of the bathroom, I was already completely deaf.

I could still see very well—I saw perfectly Sebastião's expression as he leaned over me, moving his mouth, saying things I could no longer hear.

I tried to speak, but it only produced a spasm.

Then Sebastião picked me up in his arms, one arm on my back, the other holding my leg. I felt the veins in my forehead, my neck, the shooting pulses. I didn't need to touch them to feel the uncontrolled beating.

When Sebastião left the room with me in his arms, my eyes couldn't stand the brightness of the sun and shut. After the shock I reopened them and realized that I was seeing everything upside down because my head was hanging backward.

I knew Sebastião was walking—I had all my normal senses, but could no longer hear.

The world had become mute. Only silence. But I saw everything well, even with my head hanging back I could see the black calf grazing in an open field, I could see a dog running behind the hooves of a horse pulling a cart, I could see the immensity of the white sands.

Sebastião sat me down in the sand. He stayed at my side, one of his hands firm on my neck.

Sebastião looked at the sea. So did I. The dark sea of the South.

Then he turned his head to the side and looked at me. In the movement of his lips I could read only the word *sea*.

Then I was blind: I could no longer see the sea or Sebastião.

I could only breathe deep breaths.

And I found I was ready to take, little by little, all the air into my lungs.

In those seconds, as I filled my lungs with air, I felt Sebastião's hand press mine.

*Sebastião is strong,* I thought. And I began to release the air, slowly, very slowly, until the end.

JOÃO GILBERTO NOLL is the author of nearly twenty books. His work has appeared in Brazil's leading periodicals, and he has been a guest of the Rockefeller Foundation, King's College London, and the University of California at Berkeley, as well as a Guggenheim Fellow. A five-time recipient of the Prêmio Jabuti, he lives in Porto Alegre, Brazil.

ADAM MORRIS was the recipient of the 2012 Susan Sontag Foundation Prize in literary translation. He is the translator of João Gilberto Noll's *Quiet Creature on the Corner*, also from Two Lines Press, and Hilda Hilst's *With My Dog-Eyes* (Melville House Books, 2014). His writing and translations have been published widely. He lives in San Francisco.